CW01213300

Training Amy

Anne O'Connell

Midnight Fantasy Press

Midnight Fantasy Press
U.S.A.
First Paperback Printing February 2011
Cover Art By Prism
Copyright © Stephanie Connolly-Reisner 2011
All Rights Reserved

ISBN-13: 978-1456588946
ISBN-10: 145658894X

No part of this publication may be reproduced, stored in or introduced into a retrieval system, or transmitted, in any form, by any means (electronic, mechanical, photocopied, recorded, or otherwise) without prior written permission from both the publisher and the copyright holder listed above.

This is a work of fiction. Names, characters, places, and incidents are either the product of the author's imagination or are used fictitiously, and any resemblance to actual persons, living or dead, business establishments, events, or locales, is entirely coincidental.

The publisher does not have any control over and does not assume any responsibility for author websites or third party content.

If you purchased this book without a cover you should be aware that this book is stolen property. It was reported as unsold or destroyed to the publisher and neither the author or publisher have received payment for this book.

The scanning, uploading, and distribution of this book via the internet or via any other means without the permission of the author or publisher is illegal and punishable by law. Please purchase only authorized electronic editions and do not participate in or encourage electronic piracy of copyrighted materials. Your support of the author's rights is appreciated.

Dear Reader, I tend to write my Doms and Dommes as real people with real emotions. They do feel love for and have a psychological attraction to their subs. They can also be friendly, playful, and warm. I know some readers don't like this and have complained about this with some of my previous novellas such as *Weekend Captive*. I just can't write about emotionless, loveless sexual relationships. I suppose there are other writers out there who can and do. I'm just not one of them. I also realize that in real life people may not fall in love with one another, or come to trust one another, as quickly as they may in my stories. Please remember my stories are works of fiction. Thank you for reading.

Warmest Wishes
- Anne

Chapter One

Paul fumbled around with her bra, poking her hard in the back. He pulled at the catch in futility. "Damn thing won't come off!"

Amy groaned, undoing the clasp herself. Sliding it off, she resumed kissing his neck. She felt his swollen cock on her thigh.

He immediately lifted her short black skirt. Slipping his hand down her panties he squeezed her ass. "Get these off."

That did it, she was annoyed. This was the fourth time in the past two weeks he just wanted to get her naked and stick it in without foreplay, let alone variety in positions or places. Good old missionary position in the bedroom. She pushed him away and glanced at the clock. A rush of panic ran through her. "You know what? I have to go. I have an interview in an hour."

"Babe, don't leave me like this. It will only take five minutes, I promise."

She let out a laugh before she could stop herself. Evidently he thought the usual eight minutes was a treat? She started wondering again why she was dating him. They rarely did anything fun anymore. They didn't talk. Now, all their dates led to sex – and it wasn't even good sex. Of course he was only the second guy she'd ever been with, so she wasn't really sure what good sex was, but it had to be better than this. In her imagination it was.

"Paul," she protested. "I really have to go. Maybe later tonight? Just take a cold shower or something."

She straightened herself up, put her bra and blouse back on, put the black heels back on and headed out the door with her suit jacket and bag in hand. Paul was safe, reliable and predictable. All the things her parents wanted in a potential son-in-law. He was also a law student and got good grades. He'd have a real money-making career once he passed the bar exams. With a wry smile she wondered, *what good is money if you're bad in bed?*

It was her sixth interview this week. So far the only offer she'd gotten was from some sleazy guy who told her he'd pay her seven bucks an hour plus tips to serve drinks at a local strip club. Of course once he found out she refused to go topless he retracted the offer. Now, at twenty-one, she was stuck living in her parents' basement, going to community college part time, and trying to find a job. The bus pulled up to sixth and Marquis Avenue and she got off, carefully looking around the unfamiliar street. She had filled out the application online and was honestly surprised when they called her for an interview.

Lifting her chin, she began walking down the street looking for the address. It took her a few minutes but finally she saw the sign that said, *By The Book*. With a deep breath she straightened her suit, worried quickly if she was overdressed or if her skirt was too short or her heels too high, then put on her most confident smile and headed toward the door. The outside of the shop was neat and tidy and the shop windows were clean. The inside window displays stood filled with the week's most popular books. Opening the door she was surprised to find herself greeted by the scent of fresh coffee and that new book smell. The store itself was neat and clean inside, too. The floors were spotless and the shelves well kept. A few customers wandered through the stacks and an older man was sitting in a chair off to the side of the stacks reading a history book about World War II.

If she could just get this job it would help her out tremendously. Maybe even put her that much closer to getting out of her parents' basement. Besides, she loved to read and she'd worked retail before. She walked up to the counter. There were two men there. The blond with the goatee stood leaning on the counter watching the customers and another with dark brown shoulder length hair sat typing something at a computer. They both looked to be in their thirties and both were attractive (in her opinion at least), well-built, and dressed very casually in jeans and t-shirts. A sinking feeling started in her stomach. This couldn't seriously be happening. She quickly decided she was *way* overdressed. Trying to ignore the feeling of defeat she smiled, realizing she already had the blond's attention.

"Umm, hi, I'm Amy Myers. I'm here for the interview with Brad?" She was pretty sure she sounded like a dumb ass.

The man behind the counter looked her up and down and smiled. "Well, hello Amy. Brad will be with you in just a minute." He nodded toward the guy at the computer. "Brad, Amy's here."

Amy smiled and clutched her shoulder bag. *Great, the blond was a smart ass.*

The man behind the computer finished what he was doing and turned his attention to the front counter. "Amy, come back here and have a seat."

The first man opened the swinging partition and let her behind the counter. She carefully made her way around several boxes and sat in the chair across from him. It wasn't very private. If they wanted to, the customers could listen in on her interview. Of course it was this or taking off her top and serving drinks to lonely men who liked ogling women's breasts.

The man reached across the desk and shook her hand. "I'm Brad, and that's Eric. We own *By The Book*. So I see on your application that you have retail experience. Care to elaborate?"

She gave him a nervous smile. "I worked at a small clothing boutique when I was in high school. I ran the register, stocked, and did general store cleanup. Then my first two years of college I worked at the grocery store mostly stocking and doing inventory, but I'd sometimes run a register to help out. After that I had a few office jobs."

He nodded. "Do you like to read?"

She realized Eric was listening in, too. "I love to read. Of course I haven't had as much time as I'd like to lately with school and all. Most everything I read is a college textbook these days."

"What's your school schedule like?" He looked at the papers sitting in front of him and started making notes.

She glanced at Eric, then back to Brad. "I have classes between eight and eleven in the morning Monday through Thursday."

"What year are you?"

"I'll have an associate degree by summer."

"In?" Brad lifted an eyebrow.

"Business." As she said it she realized how lame it sounded.

"Good. Willing to work weekends?" He made another note and glanced up at her.

She probably wasn't answering fast enough. "Yes."

"What was the last novel you read?"

The question completely caught her off guard. "Harry Potter and the Deathly Hallows," she said honestly. Hopefully it didn't sound too childish, but a lot of adults read *Harry Potter*, didn't they?

Much to her surprise he didn't laugh at her or give her a raised eyebrow like she expected. "Good books, they sell well. You did well on the basic skills test." He looked over at Eric and raised an eyebrow.

Eric had his hands crossed over his chest. He shrugged.

Brad leaned back in the chair. "So if you saw someone stealing a book, what would you do?"

"Call the police and file a report?" She could feel herself cringing so she forcibly tried to relax her expression.

A low chuckle escaped from Eric. He smiled but didn't say anything.

"What would you do if a customer asked for a book we didn't carry?" Brad continued, keeping his own expression calm and unaffected.

"Umm, order it for them if I could?" she said hopefully.

This time a wide grin spread across his face. "How much can you lift?"

"I'm sorry?" she wasn't sure she'd heard him right.

"Cases of books are heavy. How much can you lift?" he asked leaning forward.

She shrugged. "I don't know. Maybe twenty-five pounds or something? Maybe even fifty?"

He rubbed his hands together. "An irate customer comes in and demands his money back on a book. What do you do?"

She bit her lip. "Well first I'd ask what was wrong. I mean, if the customer just didn't like the book then he can't really expect a return. I've bought and read books I didn't like. But if it's damaged or something I would probably exchange it or give him a refund or whatever the store policy is."

He pursed his lips and regarded her for a moment. "A customer comes in and tells you the clerk who waited on him earlier was rude and he demands to speak to a manager."

Was that a question? She paused waiting to see if he said anything else. He just looked at her expectantly. "I would get a manager or tell him to come back when a manager was here."

"A man comes in with a gun, points it at you, and demands you give him all the money in the register," Brad said.

She caught Eric smile out of the corner of her eye. Swallowing hard she answered, "I'd give him the money, activate the silent alarm, umm, and I think that's it."

"What are your wage requirements?"

She froze. Really she just wanted a steady paycheck, hopefully more than minimum wage. "At least nine an hour," she said, realizing she was cringing again.

"Any questions?" This time, Brad lifted an eyebrow.

With both of them staring at her she was intimidated. She shook her head. "No."

The men exchanged glances again. Brad wrote something else on the paper in front of him then looked at the floor next to her with a frown. "Pick that piece of paper up and throw it in the trash."

Amy immediately grabbed the piece of trash and tossed it in the wastepaper basket Eric offered her.

"Thank you," Brad said. He stood. "We have a few more people to interview but if we decide you're the one, we'll call you."

Nausea overwhelmed her. This couldn't have gone worse. She forced a smile, "Thank you." She shook both their hands and ducked out of the shop as quickly as she could. Once she was out of the store and out of earshot she groaned. Could she have sounded any more spineless?

She walked across and down the street to the bus stop, flopping down on the bench with a defeated sigh. This sucked. There was no way she was getting *that* job. Going back over the answers to his questions she could have kicked herself. There were so many ways she could have answered differently. Why did employers have to ask those kinds of questions anyway? Again, the nausea gripped her. Swallowing was the only thing that kept her from losing her breakfast all over the sidewalk. Just then the bus pulled up. With a sigh of relief, she got on. She decided not to go back to Paul's. She was just too depressed. All she wanted to do was go home, crawl under a blanket and feel sorry for herself.

Chapter Two

"Amy, you need to call someone named Brad back. It's about a job at a bookstore," her mother said. Amy's mother and father were semi-retired and always home, or so it seemed. It made living at home that much more difficult.

Amy pulled the backpack off her shoulders and dropped it on the kitchen counter. Could they make college textbooks any heavier? It was like carrying around a cement block. The realization of what her mother said slowly sunk in. "Brad from *By The Book*?"

Her mother sat at the kitchen table reading a magazine. "I think that was it."

A swell of excitement rushed through her. "Right on! I think I have a job!" She hurried to the phone finding the message pad. Without hesitation she picked up the phone and dialed the number.

"*By The Book*, this is Eric, can I help you?" came the voice on the other end of the line.

"Hi Eric, this is Amy Myers, umm, Brad called earlier and I'm returning his call?" Oh God, why did she make everything sound like a question as if she was some brainless twit? She almost groaned aloud, but caught herself.

"Amy, good. Brad's actually not here now, but we'd like to offer you the job. It pays ten an hour and the hours are one in the afternoon to nine at night, Monday through Friday and Saturdays and Sundays from one to six. We can negotiate days off. Would that work for you?"

She did some quick calculating in her head. That was at least forty hours a week. "Umm, yeah, that's great."

"Good, can you come in this afternoon to fill out your paperwork?"

"Okay," she paused, "When will I start?"

"That's up to you. You can work to close tonight if you want, give you a jumpstart on your training."

She looked up at the clock. It was eleven thirty. She wanted to change and grab something to eat. "Yeah, I'll work to close tonight. I can be there by one," she said hopefully.

"That's fine, I'll see you then."

They said their goodbyes and she hung up, jumping up and down. "I got the job!"

Her mom gave her a smile. "I knew you'd find something. So do you have time to tell me about it?"

Amy hurried to the fridge and pulled out a yogurt. "Not much to tell really. It's a bookstore and I'm basically going to be stocking books and running the register. I might even be able to do homework if it's slow. But," she started; getting excited again, "It's at least forty hours a week and it pays ten bucks an hour!"

Then her mother asked, "Are there benefits?"

Amy shrugged. "I don't know."

"Amy," her mother started, "You're an adult now, and these are the kinds of questions you ask during an interview. Benefits are really important and once you're out of school you're off our medical insurance."

She rolled her eyes. Her mom meant well, but she was the kind of person who'd find a problem with winning the lottery. It was just like her to rain on Amy's parade and make her feel like she was still sixteen. "I'll ask when I go in today."

It didn't take her long to clean herself up, change her clothes and get to the bookstore. This time she dressed more casually in a newer pair of jeans and a scoop neck green blouse that drew out the color of her eyes. She had her long brown hair pulled into a ponytail and wore just enough makeup to give her that awake and put-together look. Finally, she had chosen a pair of black flats to complete the outfit. She didn't want to *overdo* the casual. She walked into the store realizing there were a lot more customers today. Eric was behind the counter, just like yesterday.

When he saw her he pointed to Brad's desk. "Paperwork in the white folder. Fill it out, Myers."

His voice was deep, commanding and intimidating. Stifling the urge to salute she gave him a shy smile and hurried behind the counter to the desk. It took her about an hour to fill out all the paperwork. She smiled when she got to the insurance information and application. After some consideration she signed up for the dental and vision, two things her parent's insurance plan didn't cover. "Eat your heart out, mom," she whispered under her breath.

"Pardon me?"

She jumped, realizing Brad was standing there. She put her hand to her chest. "You scared me."

He laughed. He had a sexy laugh. "What were you saying?"

She shook her head. "My mother. We had a conversation about benefits and insurance just this morning."

"Still living at home, huh?"

She gave him a tight smile. "Uh huh. It's another one of those unfortunate things about my life at the moment."

Brad sat back in his chair and looked her over. "You look more comfortable today."

"I hope this is okay," she said quickly, wondering if she went too casual.

"It's good." He gave her a reassuring smile. "Why don't you put your bag here in the cupboard and let's give you the tour."

She did as she was told and followed him first to the back.

He took her through a door behind the small office - register area and into a short hallway. There was a door to the left, a door to the right and then the hallway that led to a bigger room in the back. That room was lined with shelves stuffed with boxes. There was a door that presumably led outside and another to the left.

"So this is the store room. Books are organized by author back here. We only stock excess we don't have room for on the shelves and books we know are going to sell well. We do a full inventory once a month on a Sunday night. This month it's actually Sunday after next."

She looked around. "What's in there?" she asked, pointing to the door on the left.

He lifted an eyebrow. "That is a private stock room. No one except Eric and I are allowed in there. Same with the room to the left in the hallway. That's a private stock showroom for select customers and collectors. The other door, the one on the right side as you enter the hallway, that's a private employee only restroom. The public restroom entrance is in the store."

She gave him a tight smile. "Okay."

He led her back into the main store, out from behind the counter and into the stacks. "Children's books, magazines, calendars, journals, and datebooks are over there," he said, pointing to the left.

She looked around trying to note where things were.

"Right in front of us here, these six rows are fiction. It's sorted by genre and author." He looked at her as if making sure she was paying attention. "Then here to the right in the back, these twelve rows are non-fiction. They're sorted by topic and author. We've labeled the shelves. You'll notice we usually only keep 1-2 copies of each book on the shelves unless it's popular. We don't have the space the bigger stores have and we specialize in certain topics. For example, we've found tattoo and piercing books are popular with you younger kids. We have a good sized section. We have a large Christian section and an even larger Atheism section. Notice those two sections are separated from each other for obvious reasons. We also have a large human sexuality section," he said cautiously.

She nodded. "Okay."

"And finally to the left of Nature and Gardening is the bathroom. Notice the mirror up there. You have to watch that because if someone's going to steal, they start hanging out by the bathroom. Also, the bathroom has a key. People have to ask you for it. Make sure they don't take books in."

She just nodded, taking it all in. It was a pretty good sized store, she realized. Noticing a piece of paper on the floor she leaned over to grab it. That's when she realized how much cleavage her blouse was showing and that Brad was looking down her shirt.

He gave her a sly grin. "What I want you to do today is just go around and look at the shelves. See where things are and familiarize yourself with the store. When you're done, come back behind the counter and we'll discuss the register and certain protocols and store policies. Okay?"

She smiled. "Got it."

He turned and headed back toward the counter and she was left standing amidst the shelves of books. She decided to start in one corner and work her way around. Reading the labels on each shelf, she tried to make mental notes where each topic resided. When she got to human sexuality she marveled at how big the section was compared to others. He hadn't been lying. There were sex manuals from the *Kama Sutra* to *Joy of Sex*. Then something caught her eye. The label read *bdsm*. There were a lot of those books. There was also a section labeled *fetish*, probably about foot worship and stuff like that. The gay, lesbian, and transgendered section was also good sized. It took her about forty minutes to get through non-fiction. The fiction section was relatively typical. A lot of romance, fantasy, sci-fi and horror, but there was a huge erotica section and it was further broken down by type. Again there were books for those of different sexual orientation, those with fetishes, and bdsm, which she assumed was whips and chains. Finally, she made it over to the children's books, magazines, journals, calendars, and so on. That was probably the smallest section of the store and it looked relatively unused. Either that or it had been recently cleaned up.

"We usually don't get the kids until the evening hours and weekends," Eric said from the counter as if he'd read her mind.

"Great."

He laughed. "You don't like kids?"

"Depends how obnoxious they are and whether or not they're sticky and spreading it around," she said with a smile. She thought she heard Brad chuckle. With that she came back around the counter. "Well, I think I'm familiar with the shelves."

"Now for store policies." Brad got up from behind his desk and joined her and Eric at the counter. "First things first – we do accept returns of merchandise in new condition with a receipt no matter the reason for return. Your panic button is here. Use this if you're robbed. In case of fire, the alarm sounds automatically. Fire exits are labeled and there are fire extinguishers around the store. Try to get the customers out but don't endanger your life. Next, any private collectors or customers are by appointment only. Eric and I are the only ones who deal with the private collectors. Again, the two rooms in the back are off limits to you and the entire back is off limits to customers unless Eric or I take them back. Clear?"

"Yes, sir," she said carefully. Damn. He and Eric sounded like drill sergeants. That clipped way they both gave orders was going to take some getting used to, she decided.

"Good, we don't have a time clock, but you'll have a time card right here and you will log in and out. There will be time for breaks and if we're slow you can work on your homework. I realize I might be pushing my luck with your schedule and I know college produces a lot of homework. For the next few weeks you'll be in training until we know you're going to make it and we can leave you on your own for short periods. Most of the time one of us will be here with you. Okay?"

"Okay." She bit her lip and looked around, taking it all in.

Brad nodded to Eric. "You've got her until closing."

"Thank you," Eric said.

With that, Brad disappeared into the back and Eric showed her how to work the register. She watched him help customers. A lot of people seemed to be regulars and Eric knew many of them by name. When they were finally customer free and he was out of things to tell her she thought she'd ask him about the books.

"So I noticed there's a lot of erotica books."

He nodded as if people said that to him all the time. "The big chains don't carry a lot of that stuff, it's too controversial. And trust me, women read a lot of it. It's one of our biggest sellers."

"Yeah, I guess sex sells."

"Did you see the romance section?" He snorted. "My grandmother used to read those books by the bagful. She and my mom used to trade them."

She laughed. "I've never read a romance novel or erotica so I don't understand the appeal."

"Certainly you've read some forbidden books? The Sleeping Beauty books by Anne Rice under her pseudonym? Or *Story of O*?" he asked.

She shook her head. "No."

His look turned to disbelief. "Every woman I know has read at least one of those."

"Are they romance?"

"Not exactly. More erotic. You should read them when you get a chance."

She laughed. "Have you read them?"

"I didn't have to. One of my ex-girlfriends told me all about them." He shrugged. "You know, my ex may have left some books at my house. I'll check my shelves and bring them in for you."

Laughing and feeling a bit bold and silly she said, "You *have* read them! She left them at your house and you were bored and you read them."

He chuckled openly. "Well aren't you a brazen little brat. I think you'll fit in well here."

She gave him cheesy smile. Eric was a nice guy. She liked him. Good looking, smart, fun to talk to. Everything Paul wasn't. Of course Eric was also at least ten years her senior.

Closer to closing time, Eric had already moved her onto the register. Brad spent a great deal of the evening straightening the stacks, talking to customers, and stocking books as needed. Several customers stopped in for special orders that were stowed behind the register. It became her job to pull them.

She was marking a special order picked up when she felt a tap on her hand. Looking up, Paul was standing there. "You didn't call me. So I called and your mom answered and said you got a job. Thanks for letting me know. Thought I'd pick you up and we could go back to my place."

A sick feeling ran through her gut. She hadn't really wanted to tell Paul where she worked, let alone have him stop by. She'd have to have a talk with her mother about that. "Sorry, been busy," she said. Turning to put the special order log-book back on the shelf behind her, she rolled her eyes. This didn't go unnoticed by Eric who smirked. "Look, Paul, I don't get off for another hour so maybe you should go get some coffee or something and come back."

He was dressed in a blue button down shirt and a pair of tan Dockers with black leather dress shoes. That was his idea of casual. "I'll be back at nine-fifteen," he said. With that, he turned and left, but not without a glance back over his shoulder with a frown in Eric's direction.

"Boyfriend?" Eric asked, clearly amused.

She rolled her eyes again. "Yeah and it's not really working out. I've been thinking about dumping him."

"Oh?"

She took a dusting cloth from under the counter and began wiping down the register, the screen, the credit card terminal and the counter. "He's really exciting if you couldn't tell. I can't handle that much excitement in my life," she deadpanned.

Eric laughed. "Wow. Is that code for lousy in bed or what?"

Was she really that transparent? Her face went three shades of red. "You could say that, and add to it the fact that we never do anything fun anymore. I mean – how many guys in their early twenties walk around dressed like that unless they're a Republican or a Jehovah's Witness?"

He laughed again. "I totally understand. My ex was just like him. If you want, I'll call her and we can set them up."

She giggled. "And encourage them to breed? God no!"

Just then Brad set a stack of books on the counter with a thud. "Who are we encouraging to breed?"

"Vanilla, suit wearing Jehovah's Witnesses," Eric said in a hushed tone.

Brad smiled and shook his head a little. He smacked the stack of books he set on the counter. "I always walk in on the end of those conversations. Here, let's see what the return policy is on all of these and get rid of them. They're not selling."

Eric nodded, "Okay." He turned to her, "The joy of book returns. Here's how it works..." With that, Eric showed her how to process returns, strip the books that needed to be stripped and by the time he was done, Brad had already seen the last customer out, locked the door, put the closed sign on the door and turned off the main lights.

"So when is your Mormon boyfriend picking you up?" Brad asked.

She looked outside just in time to see Paul pull up in the black Chrysler his parents bought him when he graduated High School. "Right now evidently."

"I know who's not getting any tonight," Eric said with a snicker.

Her face flushed red again. "Umm, yeah."

"Well you better get your bag and go. He might pull a tire iron out of the trunk of that car and try to kick our asses," Brad said, trying not to laugh.

"Man, I know. He gave me that shitty look earlier, too. Doesn't that kid know I could take him out with one hand?" Eric crossed his arms over his chest and glared at Paul through the window.

Once she'd gotten her bag and wrote her time out on her timecard she took a deep breath and shook her head at all the male posturing. While it was a little bit flattering, it was kind of childish. "I'll be here by one tomorrow. Good night!"

Brad and Eric bade her goodnight and Brad let her out the front door, locking it behind her. Paul was standing there still staring down Eric through the window.

"Stop being an ass, Paul. You're gonna get me fired." She stood at the curb next to the passenger side door thinking he was at least going to open it or unlock it for her. But instead he stepped off the curb and went to the driver's side and got in. She pulled on the door handle. It was locked. He leaned over and unlocked it. She got in with a huff and put on her seatbelt, very aware that Paul was glaring at her.

"I don't think I like you working here."

She turned to him, literally seeing red. "What? Fuck you! I like it, I need the money, and you don't have a say."

"Are you going to be a bitch all night?" He was still glaring.

She rolled her eyes. "I don't know. If you're going to be an asshole, yeah. Maybe!"

"So which one of them are you fucking? The blond?"

Her eyes flew open. "Seriously? I've only worked here since one o'clock this afternoon! I'm not *doing* either of them."

"I don't know. I see my woman working with two men..." He didn't finish the sentence, just started the car.

She couldn't believe it. The idiot was actually jealous of her bosses. "Take me home," she demanded.

"You're not coming over tonight?"

She whirled around in her seat to face him. "Seriously? You just accused me of sleeping with my boss. You show up at my job and stare my boss down and you expect me to go home with you? Fuck you, Paul."

"Then get the fuck out of my car."

He might as well have slapped her across the face. If that was the way he was going to be... The thought kind of trailed off into a numb nothing. She undid the seatbelt, grabbed her bag, and jumped out of the car. "We're through," she said, slamming the door behind her. As he pulled from the curb the tires squealed.

She watched after him, seething with anger. There was a noise behind her. Turning, she saw Brad standing there holding the door open. "Come back in here and I'll give you a ride home in a minute. I have to wait for a collector."

Eric was now sitting at the desk looking through a catalogue of books. "Is she coming back in?"

"Yes I am." Amy walked back in. She plopped her bag on the counter and buried her head in her hand.

"You alright?" Brad asked.

"I'm really angry," she said.

"Take some deep breaths." He rubbed her shoulder reassuringly. Just then there was a tap at the front door. Brad hurried and opened the door, letting the older man in. He was wearing a black trench coat and had dark hair slightly graying at the temples. He was a big guy, too. She wondered if the three of them belonged to the same gym. Clearly they were all lifting weights or something. She left her head in her hands.

"Gary, you're late." Brad led the man behind the counter and toward the back room.

The man, Gary, had given her the once over as he came in and given Brad a questioning look. She'd seen him out of the corner of her eye. "I got caught up."

They disappeared into the back room.

Eric got up and joined her at the counter. "So you're going to sulk over that asshole?"

"He had the audacity to ask me which of you I was sleeping with. That's how jealous and stupid he was being. Then he told me he didn't like me working here as if he controls me or something. So I ask him to just take me home. He gets all pissed because he's not getting any and tells me to get out of the car. So I did and I told him we're through. I'm done."

"Well, you can certainly do a lot better," Eric agreed.

"I could do worse, too," she pointed out.

"You could," he said with a laugh.

"Now I feel bad. I'm totally putting Brad out. I can still catch the bus," she reached for her bag.

"No," Eric said flatly. "You can't. We don't want you sitting at the bus stop this late at night. This isn't the safest neighborhood for a woman after dark. He and I discussed it before we decided to hire you. Either he or I will take you home at night, unless you have a friend or someone to pick you up."

"What if I'm totally in the opposite direction?" she asked.

"Aren't you up by Clearview?"

She nodded, "Yes."

"That's right on the way home for both of us," he assured her. "I'd just take you home now but I have to pick up a friend at ten. So you get Brad tonight."

She kind of laughed.

"What's funny?" he asked.

"Any bets Paul is sitting outside my house waiting for me to get home to see how I get home?" Stifling a yawn, she pulled at her pony tail, tightening the band.

"If that's the case, I dare you to just tell him Brad was the best lay you ever had. Then the guy will go berserk on Brad and Brad will kick his ass," Eric suggested.

"Brad doesn't strike me as the violent type," she said honestly.

"He's not, usually. Under the right circumstances, however, a guy like Paul would be wise to shut up and walk away. Though I suspect Paul's not the wise type," Eric finished.

"I'm sorry," she apologized. "My first day of work and you two have already been dragged into my man-drama."

"Don't worry about it. We all have drama. Admittedly there's more of it at your age than ours, but we understood that when we hired you, too," he gave her another reassuring smile. "You did the right thing though. You kicked him to the curb, declared your independence from the drama, and joined the rest of us in the adult world. Life is too short to waste your time on people who aren't on your side and who don't care about you. I mean, look at the guy. The minute he knew you weren't going home with him, he kicked you out of the car. That's a self-serving-son-of-a-bitch right there."

"You're not making me feel any better, Eric." She heard some talking in the hallway as Brad and Gary came back out.

Gary was now carrying a plain brown bag with something in it. He had intimidating eyes. Much like Brad and Eric both did when they'd stared her down during her interview. She looked down as he passed. "This is Amy then?"

Brad nodded. "Yes, this is Amy. Amy, this is Gary, he's one of our private collectors."

Gary held out a hand.

She took it and made sure to give him a firm shake. "It's nice to meet you, Gary."

He seemed very amused and looked her up and down with narrowed eyes. "Likewise, Amy. I'll see you all later."

Once Gary was gone, Eric left to pick up his friend and Brad checked all the doors again and they left the store out the back and set the alarm. He led her to a black SUV, unlocked the passenger door and opened it for her. When she was in he closed the door.

She watched him walk around to the driver's side. He got in, pausing to put on his seatbelt.

"Did Eric tell you we don't want you waiting for the bus at night around here? It's not safe. I'm going to have to insist we'll have to take you home at night unless you can get a friend or family member to pick you up," Brad said in that practical tone he seemed to use often.

"He did," she said. "He said my house is on you guys' way home anyway."

Nodding he said, "Good, I'm glad you're not protesting."

There was no way she was protesting. She suspected it wouldn't work anyway. Noticing an uncomfortable silence, since she and Brad didn't seem to share the same rapport as she and Eric did, she took the opportunity to change the subject. "So that Gary guy, you all go to the same gym or something?"

Brad actually smiled. "Well yes, something like that."

She refrained from looking too pleased with herself. The fact that she'd pegged them did give her a boost of confidence to keep the conversation going. "Do a lot of gym-going guys actually read?"

Shrugging, he turned onto one of the main streets and headed north. "I don't know about that. But a lot of my *friends* do."

If there was a conversational roadblock, she'd just hit it, or created it. She wasn't sure which. "So Eric is bringing me in some books to borrow. Something about a *Story of O* and *The Claiming of Sleeping Beauty* by Anne Rice or something. What do you think of them? Are there vampires in the Anne Rice one? Because I am so tired of vampire books and movies and TV shows." She realized she was rambling so she shut up.

He let out an exasperated sigh and shook his head. "That's Eric for you. Right to the point."

Not knowing what to say, she merely gave him a quizzical look.

Noticing this he said, "I'm pretty sure you probably would *not* like those books."

"Why do you say that?"

Brad let out something that sounded like a muffled laugh and mutter at the same time. "They're erotic books."

"Yeah, erotic romance," she clarified.

"No." His tone was sharp and direct. "Not exactly. You'll see."

She decided to change the subject. "Thanks for taking me home. I'll talk to my mom and my friends and see if they can pick me up most nights."

"It's really not a problem at all. We're almost there," he pointed out.

He wasn't lying, a few more turns and they'd be there. That's when it occurred to her she hadn't given him an address. "You want to take a right up here."

"Yeah, I know. Navigation system," he said pointing to the display on the dash. It had been turned toward him so she hadn't really paid much attention. "I plugged in your address earlier because I thought I was taking you home before your friend showed up."

A slow smile spread across her face. He really was one of *those* types. Brad was the kind of guy who was meticulous and took care of everything.

When they finally pulled up in the front of Amy's, she looked around for the familiar black Chrysler her now ex drove. It was nowhere to be seen. She breathed an audible sigh of relief.

"We'll see you tomorrow at one," Brad said simply, all business again.

She nodded and gave him a shy smile, looking away quickly when his eyes met hers, "Thank you for driving me home."

She didn't notice the pleased grin that fell over his face. Instead, she practically ran to the front door. Something about the way Brad was, just his demeanor, intimidated the hell out of her. He waited until she got in the door before driving away.

Chapter Three

Amy poured herself a cup of coffee from the carafe and sat at the register. She'd been working at *By The Book* for two weeks now and she loved it. Eric and Brad were great bosses and always good for interesting conversation. They'd even indulged her and discussed business ethics at great length the day before. Today she was tired, and why not? After getting home last night she'd read forty pages and written part of an essay for her business ethics class, hence the previous day's conversation. Then she'd had class that morning.

Brad was fixing a window display and talking to some women about the latest stream of political books coming out of the most recent presidential administration.

Eric emerged from the back with a box of books. Plopping it on the floor he expertly pulled out a box cutter and had the box open in a few slices. He began piling them on the counter. "Help me sort these into stacks by genre. This is our small press and indie order."

Thumbing through the books she started stacks for fantasy and science fiction, romance, horror, and mystery. Stacking them neatly with spines facing her she caught Eric snickering out of the corner of her eye. "What?"

"You're a compulsive neat freak, aren't you?" He snickered again.

"Am not," she protested with a mock pout.

"I bet if I sent you into the stacks right now, in about an hour those shelves would be the neatest and straightest they've been since we opened this place," he said with a wide grin.

She gave him a playful smirk and swatted at him with a thriller novel called *Outer Darkness* by some obscure author named Audrey Brice.

He laughed.

Grabbing *Blood of the Dark Moon* by Adrianne Brennan she quickly realized some of the novels were cross genre. "Horror or romance?"

"Paranormal romance," he said quickly, then moved *Outer Darkness* from the horror pile into its own, "Paranormal mystery."

She moved them both into one pile. "How about we just say paranormal?"

He shrugged. "I suppose, but you'll have to separate them on the shelf because that's how Brad has the shelves labeled."

"How do you know anyway? Have you even heard of any of these authors?" She grabbed three more from the to-be-sorted stack. "I mean who's Selena Kitt? And I've never heard of Gail Cleare either. Bernadette Marie?"

"The first one is erotica, very popular actually, and Cleare is contemporary magic realism slash romance, and the latter is romance," he said, emptying the box. "I know this because some of it I've read, others Brad and I know the authors, and really a lot of it is popular underground stuff."

Finishing the sort took a few more minutes with Eric's help. Then she sorted them by author last name. "So should I start putting these on the shelves?"

"In a minute. Here, take these home tonight. They're the books I was telling you about when you started. I almost forgot them." He handed her three paperbacks.

"Oh, thanks!" Without really looking at them took them she tucked them away in her bag and got back to the register in time to help a customer check out.

She loved finding time to chat with Eric. To say she had a crush would have been an understatement. Once the customer was gone they sat quietly for a few minutes. She realized Eric was looking at her arms.

"What are those scars on your arms?" he finally asked.

Wondering how long he'd wanted to ask that, Amy pulled her arms behind her back. "Nothing really."

"That's not nothing." Eric caught her arm with his hand, inspecting the small half-moon shaped scars that lined her forearms.

She was uncomfortable. She never expected she'd have to explain them to anyone. Of course that was a long time ago. She hadn't hurt herself in years, but then she hadn't needed to cry for some time anyway. She was a stronger person now.

He gently ran his fingers over her scars. He wasn't stupid; he knew exactly what they were from. "So why were you digging your nails into your arm?"

She chewed at her lip, marveling at how good his touch felt. Focusing she said, "Growing up I was never allowed to cry. My parents weren't the most sympathetic people in the world. They're still not." She shrugged as if it wasn't a big thing. "So it kind of got to a point where I didn't cry because I'd get yelled at for it. I don't know, maybe I forgot how or something. Then when I was a teenager I had so many bottled up emotions that I'd go numb for days and feel like I was drowning inside myself and the only way to stop it was to dig my nails into my arms until I drew blood. The pain - it would help me cry and let it out. I used a razor blade on my leg a few times, but my mom caught me and sent me to a shrink. I went to him for about two years. I'm past that now."

Eric was quiet for a minute. "Sorry if that was an uncomfortable memory. But that explains some things. So what do you do now?"

"I don't cry. But then I don't need to cry," she told him, not exactly sure what he mean by the 'that explains some things' comment. She decided not to ask.

A deep look of concern passed over his face. "What if something really bad happens and you need to cry? Like someone you love dies? Do Brad and I need to be concerned you'll hurt yourself?"

The thought hadn't occurred to her in some time. What would she do if she needed to cry? Would she hurt herself? She looked into the darkness within and shuddered. She knew what she would do, but she wasn't telling him.

"Amy? I asked you a question. Do you ever want to hurt yourself?" Eric took a step toward her.

"I'm not a weak person like that anymore," she said simply, forcing a smile. She took a step away from him. "I wouldn't hurt myself."

The statement sounded hollow, even to her. Not to mention Eric looked entirely unconvinced. He knew she was hiding something dark and she wondered how long she'd be able to keep it a secret working here. Brad and Eric always seemed to find ways to get her to open up and relax around them. Sooner or later they'd both figure out there was something really wrong with her. Thank goodness a customer stepped up to the register.

Eric dropped it. He disappeared into the back. Brad came up to the counter, leaning on it. He looked at his watch.

"Bored?" She kind of laughed. She'd never seen the boss look at his watch before. "Or a hot date?"

He smiled. "Unfortunately bored."

She decided to be bold. "So you and Eric are both single?"

Turning to her, a small smile played on his lips, but vanished. "Yeah."

He really wasn't giving her anything to work with, like usual. "I just find that hard to believe."

"Why?"

"Well, you're both reasonably attractive. Nothing really wrong with either of you or am I missing something?"

He chuckled. "It's not like I don't date on occasion. I'm just picky."

"And Eric?"

Brad lifted an eyebrow. "You interested?"

She blushed. "I'm just curious why he's single."

"You're single."

A deep sigh emerged from her lips. "Well yeah, now I am. But I was in a relationship with a jerk up until recently if you remember."

Brad nodded as if to say she had a point. "Eric doesn't really date that often. It's taken him some time to get over his ex. He doesn't want to make that mistake again."

"Let me guess, left him for another man?"

"Not exactly," Brad said. "They were both in the same relationship, but their perception of that relationship was different. Eric was in it for the long haul and Em was just having a good time and using Eric for everything he was worth."

"Ah, he was more serious than she was?"

"Pretty much," Brad shrugged. "It wasn't meant to be. So as a result you'll find Eric has high standards for the women he dates. He's only been out with a couple of women since then and it was only dinner and a movie and he never saw them again. I think he's become an apt bullshit detector in his old age."

She laughed. "Like how old? You're both like early thirties or something?"

A huge grin spread over Brad's face. "Thank you. That's one hell of a compliment. I'm forty-two. Eric's thirty-eight."

Giving him her best look of disbelief she said, "You're pulling my chain."

"Wouldn't that be somethin'?" He gave her a smile. Just then a customer approached him, pulling his attention away from the Amy.

Once Eric came up from the back, he took the register and she spent the rest of the day restocking books and straightening shelves. A lot of customers didn't bother putting books back exactly where they found them, which she found somewhat annoying. Especially when they left the baby care books in the horror novels, which was amusing, but still annoying. By the time five o'clock rolled around she was starving.

"Amy," Brad called out from his desk in his gruff drill sergeant voice.

She jumped, dropping two of the magazines from the stack she had. Setting them down she hurried over to the corner. "Yes Sir?"

His expression softened and his eyes seemed to light up a little when he saw her. "We're getting delivery take-out from the deli for dinner. What do you want?"

Out of the corner of her eye she caught Eric give Brad a certain look. She wasn't quite sure what the look was, but it was knowing; as if they shared some secret or conversation about her. They'd been doing it since she started and it kind of bothered her. She told him what she wanted then went back to work. While they ate a few customers came through and the conversation changed to sports and she tuned it out, concentrating instead on how nice the store was looking.

That's when *she* walked in. The woman was decked out in black latex pants and patent leather spiked heels and if her cleavage had been any more ample it would have fallen out of her tight black blouse. She had long slicked back auburn hair pulled tight into a pony tail, red lipstick to match her perfect red nails and she was wearing dark sunglasses despite the fact that it was already dark. Some eighties tune, she didn't recall who sang it since it was before her time, about wearing sunglasses at night ran through her mind. Focusing, she regained control over her expression.

The woman, who oozed a great deal of confidence, breezed to the counter and only regarded Amy with a brief glance. "Hello, Brad, dear."

"Kali," he greeted.

Amy almost rolled her eyes, but stopped herself. It figured the dragon lady would go by a name like Kali. *Wasn't that a Hindu goddess of destruction?* She wondered. She'd have to look it up online later.

The woman let herself back behind the counter and gave Eric a wordless hug. "So do you have my full order?"

"I left you a message saying I did," Brad said, still cool and composed. He got up. "It's in the back. Should be enough room for you to try it all out."

She pouted. "Too bad I didn't bring Mike. Any takers?"

Eric put up his hands in mock surrender. ""Don't look at me. Only in your wildest dreams."

She threw her head back and laughed then gave Brad a narrowed look.

Brad shook his head. "Don't look at me like that woman."

Kali turned and looked expectantly at Amy. At that point, Amy felt outnumbered and intimidated and wished there was a place she could hide. "No?" Kali asked. Then she turned to Brad and Eric with a raised eyebrow.

Eric had one of those don't-talk-about-this-around-her looks on his face. Brad shook his head. "No. Amy is our shop assistant and she only deals with the books."

"Pity," Kali said, looking Amy up and down again. "Oh well, I suppose I can give it a go without a test subject."

"Come on back." He and Kali slipped into the back.

Eric visibly relaxed. "Dommes," he muttered under his breath.

Amy gave him a puzzled look. "What?"

"Nothing," he gave her shoulder a reassuring squeeze. "Don't pay any attention. Some of our private collectors and special customers are a bit eccentric. If any of them ever give you any trouble and one of us isn't right here, just tell them you only deal with the merchandise out here and then immediately grab either me or Brad, okay?"

"Okay." Her mind raced with what they could possibly be selling in the back that first off, required testing, and second, would bring in interesting characters like Kali and that motorcycle gang looking guy from that first night she'd worked here. Since she couldn't come up with anything she decided to ask. "So what exactly are you guys selling in the back rooms?"

He gave her a look that told her she was treading on forbidden ground.

She gave him a smile, knowing Eric wasn't nearly as scary as Brad, and if she could charm him enough he'd at least give her a clue. "Okay, so it's clearly not books. Neither of you look like drug dealers and neither do your clients but they do look a little," she paused, searching for the right word. "Scary," she finished thoughtfully.

He laughed. "Actually, some of it is rare, out of print books. Some of it is imported merchandise or specialty stuff."

"What's *she* here for then?" She looked at the door leading to the back room when she heard a pop noise.

"Furniture and *specialty* items," Eric said carefully. He handed her a phone order sheet. "Here, go pull these books for this order. The woman is going to be in for them tomorrow."

She took the list just as the door to the back swung open and Kali breezed out.

"It's perfect, Eric. You and Brad always take care of me." She kissed him on the cheek, leaving a little red lipstick there. She wiped at his cheek. "So here is my receipt. Brad is taking it out the back and loading it in my friend's car. Where did you find it?"

Amy buried her nose in the list and pretended to look it over.

Eric went to the cash register and started ringing Kali up. "We have a guy in Bridgeport who makes it all by hand. That will be thirteen-hundred-forty-two and sixteen cents."

Amy thought she was going to choke on her own disbelief but held herself steady, regarding the list even longer. Once she was certain she was lingering too long, she cautiously made her way out from behind the counter and went into stacks to pull the books on the list. Concentrating on her task was easy. The first two books were on the erotica shelf and both were in stock. She flushed red when she realized the rest of the books were in the bdsm non-fiction section. She pulled each title carefully, curiously sneaking a look into the books only to see pictures of women bound by ropes and suspended in air, along with pictures of sex toys. A male customer was browsing the political section in the next aisle. Swallowing, hard, she closed the book she was looking at in a panic realizing the pictures of the bound women inside excited her.

Not seeing them bound per se, but imagining *being* bound up like they were. After a few minutes she was able to compose herself, finish pulling the rest of the list, and take it back to the counter. By this time Kali and her furniture were gone. She stifled a smile. Books and made-to-order specialty furniture, it was an odd combination.

Going through the list quickly, Eric checked to make sure everything was there. Once again, Brad was behind the desk looking at the computer. "Eric, take a look." He turned the monitor toward Eric.

"Oh, nice," said Eric.

She rolled her eyes when she saw what they were looking at. "Custom built saw horses? Seriously? Why is the top padded?"

Both men burst into laughter.

"To keep the wood from getting scuffed," Brad said with a chuckle.

Eric broke out laughing again.

Men. It always amazed her how seriously they took their tools and shop equipment. She shook her head and went back to the non-fiction section to straighten up a shelf she noticed earlier that someone had already messed up.

Nine o'clock came quickly. Since she still had no one able to pick her up, tonight it was Eric who drove her home. He drove a restored '65 black Mustang with a leather interior.

Once they were both seat-belted in, he turned to her. "Ready?"

Her eyes went wide. "Are you going to drive like an asshole?"

He laughed. "No, I'll drive carefully. But I sometimes have to, you know, work the bugs out of the engine by flooring it." With that, he pulled out of the parking lot onto the street. "You'll have to tell me where to go since Brad has had the pleasure of taking you home regularly for two weeks now."

Conversation was tremendously easier with Eric. "So how did you get into selling furniture?"

He laughed again. "It's just something we do."

"What kind of furniture?"

He seemed to think about this for a moment. "Specialty stuff."

Then it hit her. "Oh, like theme stuff? I have a girlfriend who is really into the middle-ages and she had to order some cross frame chairs from a place in Chicago."

"Exactly like that," he agreed. "We just have a lot of local customers who prefer to buy it from us. People who frequent our club," he stopped dead then tried to change the subject. "So straight on Sycamore, then a right at sixty-eighth?"

"Yeah," she said. No, it hadn't gone unnoticed that he changed the subject. "You guys have a club?"

"Just a private thing we have on the side with a few other friends. They run it, we're just investors really." He turned strangely silent.

She knew she should probably just leave it alone and so she did. "So my parents go to bed at eight-thirty every night and my friends are all blowing me off so it might take me a bit longer to arrange a steady ride than I'd hoped..."

"That's okay," he said brightly. "I don't mind driving you home. I'm pretty sure Brad doesn't mind either."

That's when she recalled the look Eric had given Brad earlier. "So am I doing a good job?"

"Of course, why?" he looked over at her with a bit of concern. "Did you think maybe we didn't think you were doing well? Because I assure you you're doing great. We have plans to keep you as long as we can. Having you around is going to mean Brad and I can take more time off."

She yawned but didn't want to stop the conversation. "So was Brad ever in the military?"

"Marines actually, before college. Why?" Eric gave her a quick sidelong glance.

"He's always so," she paused, trying to find the right word. "Commanding?"

"Brad is a very in-your-face kind of guy. But you always know exactly what he expects and where you stand with him, right? He's also fair and honest and one of the nicest people I know. I couldn't have a better friend," he said.

"I didn't mean anything by it. I like Brad. I was just curious. He has a very orderly, always prepared, practical, military thing going on. And he sounds like a drill sergeant sometimes. That's all," she said with a quick smile, worried she might have again treaded on forbidden territory yet again. She was famous for doing that.

Eric chuckled. "Yeah, he is very much like that. That doesn't scare you does it?"

Shaking her head she said honestly, "It will take some getting used to but really it makes me want to call him *Sir* and salute."

A full belly laugh came out of Eric. "Wow. That's funny. I have to tell him that."

Panic flooded her. "No, don't tell him that, he'll want to fire me."

"Doubtful. Last I heard he was already planning the schedule through next year. He does have a sense of humor, you know. He just isn't as open with it as I am with mine.

Once you get to know him better you'll see." He gave her another reassuring smile.

Then they began talking about movies and before she knew it, they were in front of her house. She hated it when that happened. There were days she wished work never ended just so she could talk to Eric. Now, she was wishing the ride home was longer. "Thanks for the ride. I'll see you tomorrow at one again." She gave him a sweet smile. She really did like Eric despite the fact he was older. A lot older, she'd discovered. Of course he probably wasn't interested in some twenty-nothing college girl, but it didn't keep her from flirting.

"Alright. Get some sleep. Maybe read a book, relax. That will help." He flashed that brilliant smile at her.

She closed the car door and hurried up to the house, unlocked the door and waved before going inside. He waved back, but waited to pull away from the curb until she was safely inside. Closing the door behind her, and locking it, she went straight to the kitchen to grab a soda. Then, giant bag of books in tow, she descended into the basement and threw herself onto the bed, exhausted.

But she couldn't sleep. She was going to have to wind down first. Looking warily at the can of caffeine-free soda in her hand she sat up, set the soda on the bedside table and opened her book bag. The three books Eric had given her were sitting on top. She took them out, setting them on the headboard. Maybe she would read. She reached back and grabbed the books again and looked at them. One was called *Story of O* by Pauline Reage. Another was *The Claiming of Sleeping Beauty* by A. N. Roquelaure, and finally there was one called *Carrie's Story* by Molly Weatherfield. They were all dog-eared as if they'd been well read. The first two had boring covers. The third, however, had a mostly naked woman's backside on it. That's the one she decided to start with. She was a relatively fast reader and the book wasn't too long.

Settling in she began reading. As she read she found herself getting warm and felt the familiar tingling of arousal between her legs. She paused long enough to strip down to her underwear and continued reading. It was tempting to rub herself off, but she refrained. She wanted to know what happened. Before she knew it, she'd finished the book and it was only eleven-forty-five. Her nimble fingers slid between her thighs, finding her clit. Starting slow, she rubbed herself, increasing speed as the fantasy of Eric tying her up and licking her clit ran through her mind. She could imagine him flogging her ass. Oh God he was beautiful. She wondered how big his cock was and what it would feel like buried deep inside her. As she came, she lifted her hips, imagining them meeting his.

She took a few deep breaths. Looking at the clock she decided she had time to read another. Next, she picked up *Story of O*. Once again, some of the acts and images the books evoked sent warmth and arousal through her. Enough so that she took the dildo she kept hidden in the closet out of its box and ran it over her clit as she read, bringing herself just to the brink of orgasm, then stopping to read some more. Some of what she read repulsed her. It was too far over the top, but when a particular scene aroused her, she savored it, masturbating herself until she came. The flesh between her legs was sticky and wet - wanting. When she was done she realized it was too late to read the third. It was already almost two in the morning. She couldn't help but wonder why Eric had loaned the books to her. These weren't just erotic stories; they were downright kinky and somewhat scary. Scary in the fact that some of what the books described turned her on so much that just thinking about it, and putting herself and Eric into the story, she almost came without any stimulation to her clit at all. Nothing had ever made her feel this aroused before.

She looked at the clock warily. Her only class the next morning was a management practicum and the professor followed the book religiously. She could read and catch up. With a final glance at the clock she picked up *The Claiming of Sleeping Beauty*. By the time she finished reading it was five-thirty in the morning and her sheets were wet. Now she knew why Brad had reacted the way he did. What had he said? She tried to remember. That's Eric, right to the point or something like that? What did that mean?

She began wondering if Eric was into bdsm. Did he like to tie women up? Spank them? The mere thought sent a shiver of excitement through her. She bit her lip and took a deep breath. As far as she saw it she had two choices. She could take a shower and stay up (considering her heart was pounding in her chest at all the sexual thoughts of Eric tying her up and using a flogger on her), or she could go to bed, feign illness for the morning, and get up by eleven so she could get to work by one.

She debated bringing the books in with her the next day to give them back, but decided it was too soon. She didn't want Eric to know that the books interested her enough that she'd been greedy and read all three in one sitting, sacrificing sleep to do so. No, she'd wait at least a week then casually bring them back as if they hadn't surprised her at all. Then she could just say, "They were interesting," and leave it at that. After all, she wasn't discussing bdsm with her boss. That was just unprofessional. Of course so was flirting with him and so was fantasizing about him.

With that she set the alarm for eleven, turned out the light, and went to sleep.

Chapter Four

She didn't feel the least bit guilty about ditching her class that morning and the bus ride in had been comfortable enough. She sat behind the register watching over the customers with a wide grin. Customer service had always been one of her strong suits. In every job she ever had she always made good marks on that during reviews. Eric was out that afternoon, thank God. She wasn't sure she could look at him after reading those novels and the fantasies she'd had about him. Just thinking about it made her draw her thighs together in response to the immediate arousal. The last thing she needed was to get aroused at work by thinking about her boss. Of course Brad and Eric didn't feel so much like bosses. Instead, it was like working for friends and she didn't mind going that extra mile to please them. If that meant being tidy and always on time and following orders to the letter, that's what it meant.

Feeling like she was being watched, she turned around only to catch Brad regarding her thoughtfully.

"Drill Sergeant, eh?" He actually smiled at her and shook his head.

She immediately turned six shades of red and wanted to crawl under a rock. "I can't believe he told you I said that."

With an open laugh Brad leaned back in his chair. "I'm just very goal oriented. Things need to get done and I've found dealing with most things in the most direct manner possible is the best way to proceed. Now, speaking of, you seem overly contemplative today. What's up?"

"I, uh, nothing really."

"Still problems with that Paul guy?"

He'd actually remembered Paul's name. With nervous energy she grabbed the rag from under the counter and wiped down the counter, the register, and the credit card terminal. "No, I just, it's nothing."

"When you get nervous, you clean obsessively. Did you know that?" He pointed to the rag her in hand.

She smiled and set the rag down. He was right and obviously very observant.

"You read one of those books he loaned you."

Mortified she tried to say something, but the words wouldn't come out. How did he know?

"That's a big yes if I've ever seen one. Guess it's a good thing Eric isn't here, huh? Awkward." Brad sucked a deep breath through his teeth. "I told you the night you started that I didn't think you'd like them."

She took a deep breath and looked around to make sure the customers were out of earshot then lowered her voice. It all came tumbling out. "So his ex-girlfriend left the books at his house and he loans them to me, it makes you wonder if he's into that kind of stuff. I mean the first book was... and the second I couldn't even believe... and the third one was just so... Oh my God."

Brad's eyes went wide. "You read *all three*?"

"Oh yeah." She picked up the rag and continued wiping everything down furiously.

"In one night?"

She turned to him, noting the huge grin on his face. The jig was up. That was the truth of it, wasn't it, she told herself. She *did* read *all three* of them in one night. It spoke volumes and those volumes didn't scream *dislike*. "Well, yeah, but because it was like watching a train wreck. Like I couldn't look away or like I couldn't believe what I was reading."

"So you just had to read more?" He was still smirking and then he started laughing.

That's when she realized how ridiculous and childish she sounded. "Okay, so I was fascinated and intrigued by them. I've never read anything like that. They were *interesting*."

"Well, maybe you'll consider reading more," he said carefully, regaining his calm composure.

Her mind began to race. More? "Why?" she finally asked.

"Quite frankly, I think you enjoyed it. But mostly because we have a lot of women customers who come in here for that particular type of erotica and some have asked if we had a woman in the store who could give them recommendations. I just thought if you liked it you could read more and it would be a great help to the customers," he explained quite seriously.

Well that made sense, she thought. "Oh. Maybe that's why Eric loaned them to me to begin with."

"Oh, yeah that's probably it," Brad agreed with a smirk.

A young woman about five-four with blond hair and blue eyes approached the counter. She was clearly timid. Conservatively dressed and carrying a large brown handbag she leaned in close, eying Brad warily. "I'm here to pick up an order. It's under Mary Alexander."

Her voice was so soft that if Amy hadn't been paying attention she might have had to ask the woman to repeat herself. She looked on the order shelf, found the order and pulled it. She pulled out all the books. The woman's eyes went wide.

"I just want to make sure they're all here," she said quickly, noticing the woman's obvious discomfort. Looking over the list she realized this was the erotica and bdsm order she'd pulled yesterday so she was careful to act nonchalant. Had it been her order she knew she would have been more comfortable if the clerk acted as if it was no big deal. She scanned the books, carefully placing them back in the brown *By The Book* bag. "That's fifty-nine and sixty two cents."

The woman paid with a credit card and all but ran out of the shop with her head down.

"And that's why we needed a woman working here," came Brad's voice in her right ear.

She jumped.

"Sorry, didn't mean to scare you." His hand grazed her back and the fine hairs on the back of her neck stood up in absolute pleasure as her nipples hardened.

"Do a lot of women order their porn and then pick it up later?" Amy asked, trying to shrug off the confusion coursing through her. Brad's touch was a huge turn on, but she wanted Eric.

"One man's porn is another man's pleasure. Or in this case, woman's. Let's order pizza for dinner. Eric should be back by then." Brad posted a coupon for office supplies on the corkboard. He turned to her and pointed to the coupon. "Don't let me forget that we have that, it's like twenty bucks off."

It was her turn to laugh. "Okay."

Just then Eric showed up carrying *Starbucks*. He handed one to Amy, "Mocha Latte, for you gorgeous. And a Frappuccino for you," he said, handing Brad a cup. "And one for me."

She couldn't help but feel a little surprised. How had he known she liked Mocha Latte? All he'd ever seen her drink was regular coffee with sugar and cream. "How did you know?"

"It was a guess," he said. "I almost got you Pumpkin Spice, but you seem more Mocha Latte. Did that timid little sub come get her books?"

"What?" Amy turned to him, confused.

"That Mary something," Brad said. "Yeah, she came in. Amy helped her. I thought she was going to bolt out the door."

"The guy who gets that one is going to have his work cut out for him," Eric said quietly to Brad.

But Amy had heard him. She decided not to say anything. Instead she grabbed a few books off the counter to put away. "Be back in a few, I'm going to go put these back on the shelves."

Both men watched her leave and exchanged another one of their wordless looks.

She wasn't stupid. Maybe a bit naïve, yeah, but not stupid. She'd heard him yesterday when he'd called Kali a Domme. He had called Mary Alexander a sub. The shop had an uncharacteristically large bdsm sections in both fiction and non-fiction. Eric had given her some bdsm books to read. He and Brad were part owners in a club of some sort. Putting two and two together wasn't a stretch. But to completely verify her suspicions, she had to find out what was in the back rooms – and she didn't mean the main storage room.

She returned to the register and resumed her place behind the counter helping the customers. Again, nine o'clock came quickly and again, Eric took her home. He didn't mention the books, so evidently Brad hadn't said anything. Or maybe Eric didn't want to bring it up either.

Either way it was fine with her. They mostly chatted about movies on the way home again. They were both fans of action movies.

"I thought *Alien vs. Predator* was kick ass," he was saying as they pulled up to her house.

He was so good looking. He had a sharp jaw and high cheekbones, well placed apart eyes and his face had symmetry. She also liked that he had that bad-boy look with the shoulder length blond hair. He kept it in a ponytail, but it was still hot. And he didn't always shave. Not to mention he was a big guy. She'd only seen him in t-shirts but she imagined his chest and arms were impressive. All her reservations about him had melted. There was no way the man next to her was sadistic, cruel, violent, or even a misogynist. He seemed like a normal guy. A normal guy who was really hot and who, regardless the fact that he was older, really made her feel stupid and swoony, like a teenager.

"Earth to Amy?"

A flush of red ran up her neck and into her cheeks. "Sorry, I was just thinking," she said feeling stupid.

He smiled at her. "Hey, I know this is probably really unprofessional of me, and maybe even a bit bold, but would you like to have dinner Saturday night after work?"

Her eyes went wide. "Won't Brad get mad?"

"Why, did you have dinner plans with him?" He laughed, clearly kidding.

"No," she said. "I mean won't he freak out if you and I go out outside of work?"

"He won't care."

This was almost too uncomfortable. "I don't know, is it like a friend thing or a date thing," she asked carefully, wincing like she did when she was unsure.

"Both," he said confidently.

Her mind screamed no. Her body screamed yes. Dating her boss, bad idea she quickly decided. "I don't know…"

"I understand your hesitation. Dating the boss is a bad move, right? If it doesn't work out you wonder if you still have a job and even if you do, things will be strange, all that crap. I get it," he shrugged.

"And if I say no…" she cringed again. "I really don't know. Maybe if it was just a friend thing?" she asked hopefully.

"Yeah, okay." He seemed happy with that answer.

She grabbed her bag. "I'll see you tomorrow."

She closed the car door and bolted up to the front door, letting herself in. Again, he waited until she was inside before he drove away.

That night she pulled the dildo out of its box in the closet again. She imagined Eric restraining her, kissing her neck, dragging his fingers down her bare body, over her breasts. Then she imagined him sliding his tongue between her legs, up her wet slit and over the hood of her clit. She gasped, rubbing the dildo over her swollen clit. She imagined him pinching her nipples and licking around her anus, then slipping his tongue inside her pussy to taste her. With that she pressed the dildo into her now wet hole, pushing it in further and further until it filled her. Slowly, she pulled it out imagining his cock inside her. She pushed it in again, slowly, she began working the dildo in and out of her pussy, delighting in how her clit swelled, begging to be rubbed. When she couldn't stand it anymore she began rubbing her clit in tight circles, faster and faster, thrusting the dildo in and out of herself, the latex dong penetrating her and spreading her wide open. She was so wet. It felt so good. When she came she imagined a flogger being brought down on her ass.

In the fantasy it may have been Eric fucking her, but it was Brad holding the flogger.

Once she'd cleaned herself and the toy up she tried to fall asleep, but the thought of Eric wanting to date her and her fantasies of him and the possibility of what he and Brad were into – it was too overwhelming. Finally, she did fall asleep, but it was restless at best and only made her more curious about the secrets they were hiding in the back room.

***

Friday nights at the bookstore were actually pretty busy. Brad had taken the night off, leaving Amy and Eric to run things alone.

"So you guys are alternating Friday nights off?" She asked as she marked some special orders picked up.

"That's the plan," he said, checking out what seemed like the hundredth customer in the last hour.

"This is only my third Friday here and you know I would have never guessed so many people would spend their Friday nights hanging out at a bookstore," she whispered.

He laughed. "I know, right? But, that's a good thing. It's good for business."

Things started winding down closer to nine. At eight-forty-five there were still a few customers milling about.

"Excuse me, miss," an older woman wearing a wide brimmed hat asked.

The hat took Amy by surprise. She smiled, "Yes?"

"I need to find a book for my grandson, could you help me?"

"Sure!" Amy came out from behind the counter and started leading the woman toward the children's section just as the phone began ringing. Eric answered it.

When Amy returned, Eric looked upset.

"Everything okay?"

"No actually. Umm, at nine I have to leave for about fifteen or twenty minutes and I am going to leave you here to close up. Is that okay?" He gave her a concerned look.

"That's fine," she insisted.

"I shouldn't be too long. I have to go pick up Brad. I'll come back and grab you and take you home."

A swell of panic rose in her gut. "Oh my God, is he okay?"

"Yeah, he's fine so he says, but his car isn't. Some asshole rammed him on purpose." Eric seemed genuinely pissed.

"Wow." She didn't know what else to say. "No, it's not a problem at all."

By nine the last customer had left. Eric ran a quick check through the store and the back, he even unlocked the customer bathroom and checked in there to be sure no customers were left in the store. "I'm not taking any chances you being alone in here. Stay close to the phone."

She nodded.

He handed her a set of keys. "This is just in case anything happens and you need to leave and lock up or whatever. The front is locked, the bathroom is empty and locked, and when I leave out the back I want you to lock it behind me. I have a set of keys. I'm leaving the lights on in back so we can see when we get back, okay? If you get scared or anything call me on my cell."

"Okay," she took the keys and his cell number obediently, following him to the back. Once he was gone, she locked the door behind him.

Wandering up to the front she sat down on the stool behind the counter and looked out to the street beyond, the streetlamps casting a yellowish glow over everything. After about five minutes she was really bored. She could always straighten shelves, but then she worked a full day tomorrow. There would be plenty of time to straighten shelves then. A rush of excitement raced through her when it dawned on her that tomorrow night she and Eric were going out. Her fantasies from the night before flooded back to her and she looked at the keys on the counter next to her, then at the door leading to the back room and the locked doors.

A little peek wouldn't hurt, would it? She wouldn't touch anything. No, that wasn't her style. She had ethics, after all. But she needed to know and her curiosity was just too great. With a deep breath she picked up the keys and made her way to the hallway leading to the back room. She eyed the door to her left warily and looked at the keys. Sliding one into the lock she was a bit surprised when it clicked and she was able to turn the knob with ease. She went into the room, found the light, clicked it on and almost laughed at herself. It really was just a private stock room. It smelled like old books and that's exactly what it contained; shelves and shelves of what looked to be old books and possibly first edition hardcovers. Some of them labeled that they'd been signed by the author.

With a shake of her head at her own wild imagination, she clicked off the light, closed the door and made sure she locked it behind her. She took a step back toward the front of the store when something inside her compelled her to stop. What about the furniture? She had to take a look, didn't she? After all, something a woman like Kali would buy had to be interesting. With that she hurried back to the second private stock room and quickly found the padlock key and unlocked the door. The door opened inward. This room smelled like furniture. Wood and leather. Sliding her hand against the dark wall she found the light and clicked it on, but not before running into something and knocking it over. A multitude of clanking, like sticks falling out of a bucket, resounded through the entire stock room.

"Shit," she whispered. Looking down that's exactly what it was. A multitude of sticks lay on the floor, the bucket they were in tipped over. She scooped them up and put them back into the container, setting it back where it should have been. Standing up, she surveyed the stuff in the room. There were strange looking chairs, benches, and pieces of wood. One looked like an X. She moved further into the room to get a better look, noticing all the furniture had O rings on it. She looked to the right and saw a multitude of whips hanging on the wall and she gasped.

There were so many of them in different colors and sizes and lengths. She never imagined there were so many types of whips. So, just because they sold the stuff didn't mean they were into it, she told herself. Turning, she started back toward the door, catching sight of the shelves of cupping devices, dildos, anal plugs, nipple clamps and metal bars that looked like they had shackles attached.

She heard the Mustang pull up. "Shit!" she cried out again. In a rush she ran toward the door only to trip on the canister of sticks again. The damn thing toppled over. A wave of panic and nausea ran through her. Switching off the light she pulled the door closed behind her and relocked the padlock just as she heard the key enter the back door. Bolting for the front, she jumped into the chair and tossed the keys on the desk next to her. She tried her best to look like someone who'd been patiently waiting.

"Amy?" Eric called out.

"Yeah?" She cocked her head to one side when they came through the door.

"Everything okay?"

"I was going to ask you the same question."

Brad had a scratch along his jaw.

She jumped up when she saw it. "What happened? Is this from the car accident?"

"You mean the guy who rammed me? It wasn't an accident. The guy was high on something. This wasn't from that though. This was from the asshole hitting me. I think he was wearing a ring or something. Cut me."

She grabbed the first aid kit from under the counter. "Sit down and let me get a good look at it."

"No, I'm fine."

"No, man, she's right," Eric said, nudging Brad to sit. "At least let her put some anti-bacterial on it and clean it up so it doesn't get infected."

Brad sat down with some reluctance and looked up at her.

She tipped his head up toward the light so she could see it better. It looked superficial. It wasn't deep and it had already stopped bleeding. She took a cleansing wipe to it.

"Son-of-a-bitch it stings! Ah!"

"I have to clean it out," she told him sternly. Once she was satisfied it was clean she put some anti-bacterial ointment on it. "Good job."

Eric laughed.

"What, am I five?" Brad gave her an amused look.

"I'm fresh out of lollipops," she shot back.

Eric laughed again. "Time to go home."

They all agreed. Amy handed the keys Eric had given her back to him and he took them without word.

As they left she hoped and prayed that they wouldn't pay much attention to the can of tipped over sticks. Brad let her take the passenger seat and he got in back and on the way home, he regaled her with the story of his SUV's demise and subsequently how he kicked the ass of the guy driving the other vehicle. How he'd gotten himself into that situation in the first place was conveniently left out.

Chapter Five

Saturday morning came quickly, and with it a barrage of customers who rummaged through the shelves at such speeds that Amy could scarcely keep up with keeping things neat and straightened like Brad liked them. Both she and Brad worked the floor while Eric kept himself busy at the register. A few times Brad had left to help a select customer or collector in the back. She had no way of knowing if they were legitimate book collectors or "special" customers for the stuff in the far back room. Of course she wasn't sure she wanted to know. No, she *was sure* she didn't want to know.

As she saw it she was at another crossroads. She could either freak out and act like a child and quit her job because it was possible one or both of her bosses were into kink on their own time. Or she could buck up, pull on her big girl panties and educate herself on what all the fuss was about. Especially if a large number of the customers were also interested in such reading material. After all, she didn't have to deal with what they had in the back. They'd said it themselves – she dealt with the books. That was all.

Then it hit her. She had agreed to have dinner with Eric tonight. She couldn't help but wonder if Eric was really into it. After all, he'd loaned her the books his ex-girlfriend had allegedly left at his house. A bit of nervousness ran through her. She got along with Eric famously. When she was talking with him it seemed as though they had known each other forever. He couldn't be into anything like that. He was too nice. Too normal. She relaxed a little then and reassured herself she had nothing to worry about. Dinner was just dinner. It was Brad she was uncomfortable around. He had all the charm of a prickly pear cactus. No, that wasn't fair – Brad had his own qualities and charm, she admitted to herself as she straightened the fantasy novel section. She remembered his touch and her body's reaction. Then the fantasy… It's just that Brad was a bit more sober, more practical, and fussier about the cleanliness of things.

What if that back room was *his and not Eric's*? Who was she kidding? Of course it was Brad's and Eric's too. She winced. Brad was pretty fussy about how clean things were. He was sure to notice the knocked over container of sticks. Yet neither Eric nor Brad had mentioned anything amiss in the back and she was comfortable pretending it never happened. If confronted she decided she'd just play dumb and pretend she had no idea what happened. Brad told her not to go into those rooms, after all.

Making her way back toward the non-fiction section she started straightening the human sexuality shelves. Feeling bold she grabbed what looked like an introductory book about bdsm. "Well, if I'm going to help the terrified Mary's I might as well read up, eh?" she whispered under her breath with a laugh. She flipped through the book and before she knew it, she'd read an entire chapter. The movement of a man in the next row over made her jump and put the book back on the shelf.

"Amy?" came Brad's voice from between the rows.

She hurried out of the stacks and smiled when she saw him.

"I have some orders to place and we need to give Eric a break at the register," Brad said, quickly as he moved back behind the counter. He sat down at the computer and immediately engrossed himself with whatever was on the screen.

She slipped behind the counter to the register.

"Thanks," Eric said with a smile. He picked up a stack of books from behind the counter. They looked really old.

"Oh, I finished those books you loaned me. I'll bring them back tomorrow. Thank you," she said with a polite smile. With that, she turned to help a customer who'd approached the counter with a magazine. Out of the corner of her eye she caught Brad shaking his head and Eric grinning ear to ear as he disappeared into the back room with the books.

She'd helped about six customers, one after another, when Brad ordered, "Go into the back and ask Eric what he wants on his burrito."

She looked at the register. Was it going to run itself? She saw and older woman making her way to the counter with about three books. "What about...?"

Brad jumped up and took her spot. "I'll deal with it, go."

She started toward the back. "Yes Sir."

"If you're going to say *Yes Sir*, say it like you mean it," he quipped back.

She rolled her eyes, opening the door into the hallway. There was a foreboding feeling in the air. "Eric? Where are you?"

She heard a door close. "Back here."

Entering the back stock room she saw him putting a padlock on the private stock storage room. "Master Brad would like to know what you want on your burrito. Or maybe I should call him Drill Sergeant Brad."

Eric regarded her for a minute. He wasn't smiling, at first. Then his normally playful expression returned. "What's gotten into you?"

"Guess I'm feeling a bit frisky."

"Oh?"

"Yeah. So, burrito?" She raised an eyebrow.

"I'll go up and tell him myself," he said decidedly.

Nodding in response she started back toward the door.

"Amy, hold on. I have to ask you something."

There was a tone to Eric's voice. A tone she wasn't sure she cared for. She lifted an eyebrow and turned to him. "Sure!"

"When I went to pick up Brad last night, were you snooping around in the back room?" His expression was dead serious.

She felt her face flush six shades of red and she swallowed, hard. There was no way she could lie; not to Eric. "I, umm, thought I heard movement, like rats or something."

He furrowed his brow. "Were you told not to come back here?"

Fear clutched at her gut. Great, she'd done it now. She was going to get fired and lose the hot guy all because she was too curious for her own good and couldn't be trusted. She looked down at her feet. "Yes, Sir. I'm sorry."

"This is a serious offense." He shook his head and turned back to the door, unlocking it. "Come here."

She swallowed again, pent up emotion swelling inside her, hitting that wall. Willingly her feet did as she was told. Following him into the room she waited as he pulled the cover off a large cage. A moment of puzzlement passed over her face. She didn't say anything.

He took the pin out of the cage door and turned to her with a sober expression. "Take off your clothes and get in the cage."

Disbelief overwhelmed her. "Umm, sorry?" She wasn't sure she'd heard him right. The whole thing seemed surreal.

Letting out a deep sigh Eric regarded her for a moment, grabbing a whip from a table. "You've broken the rules, Amy. The rules were not meant to be broken. Now it's time to pay the penalty for disobeying a direct order. Two hours in the cage. Clothes off, in."

A rush of excitement and fear ran through her. She wasn't sure which was stronger. Either way she felt she was going to be sick.

"Come on. I don't have all day. I need to get back up front." Eric's eyes bore into her expectantly.

"I'm not getting in there," she finally said.

"You either do as I say of your own free will or I'll bind and gag you and put you in the cage myself. Don't make this difficult."

She looked at the whip in his hand. He was certainly stronger than she was. How could she have been so wrong about him? They'd spent almost eight hours a day together for the last three weeks.

He took a step toward her.

Unbidden she kicked off her shoes and began undressing. All the while Eric watched her, seemingly emotionless and detached. When she had removed everything and stood nude in front of him with her hands over her breasts and her legs tightly clenched of course, he regarded her for a moment.

"Put your hands behind your back and spread your legs."

A warm tingle spread through her sex. With some reluctance and some embarrassment she took her hands away from her breasts and pulled them behind her back, feeling her chest naturally arch outward, shoving her full breasts forward for his inspection. Then she stepped her legs apart, painfully aware of her exposed shaven pussy.

An approving look washed over his face. "Good, now into the cage."

He motioned her into the cage and she went, feeling a rush of excitement when he closed the door behind her.

"Now get on your knees, legs spread and hands behind your back," he ordered.

Drawing in a deep breath she maneuvered in the tight space and did her best to follow his instructions. She said nothing. It was as if her voice no longer worked. Her willpower left her. She so badly wanted that look of approval from Eric. After all, he was right. She wasn't supposed to have been back here at all. She *deserved* to be punished. When that thought crossed her mind she felt her slit moisten.

He was still watching her. Quietly he set the whip on the bench then picked up her clothing and also set it on the bench. "I'll be back in two hours and I'll let you out. Stay in *the position*."

With that he simply left the room, closing the door behind him.

Once he was gone she looked down at herself. Her nipples were hard, her lips swollen and her arousal glistened between her legs. Oh God. He'd seen it all. She closed her eyes and tried to stay in *the position* wondering all the while what was going to happen when he came back. Would he demand more payment for her infringement? Would he use a whip on her? Would he fire her? She was pretty sure this meant dinner was off. Closing her eyes she concentrated on her breath, staying in *the position*.

Why was she doing this? She could sit however the hell she wanted, part of her screamed. Another part of her screamed for approval and didn't want to move. It was the latter side that was winning. Shoving the thoughts from her mind she went back to her breath, trying to ignore the fact that her pussy was dripping and she was very aroused.

Two hours felt like fifteen. When the door opened again, she breathed a sigh of relief, fighting the natural instinct to cover herself. Opening her eyes she gasped realizing it was Brad and one of his private customers.

He merely glanced at her with a smirk and led the customer, a distinguished man wearing a suit, maybe fifty or so, into the room. "The furniture is made by a man a few counties over in his home woodshop. All of it is customizable if you wish."

"Very nice spanking benches," the man said, running a well-manicured hand over the leather cushion of the bench. "How much?"

The man didn't look at Brad, instead he looked around the room, his eyes settling on Amy for a moment then moving to the wall of whips.

Brad watched his customers' gaze carefully, "Two hundred and fifty."

The customer's gaze settled on Amy then. Or at least it seemed like he was looking at her. "Nice cage. What's it made out of?"

"Steel. They're fully collapsible. Unpainted, thirteen-hundred," Brad said. He gave her a wink.

Amy looked down, trying to disappear.

But the customer's attention then went to the back wall. "Ah, spreader bars. I need another one for the house slave. Cost?"

"They range from seventy-five to two-fifty," Brad said, sounding somewhat bored.

"Good. I'll take a cage, that bench over there, and two of those spreader bars. I might consider one of those Saint Andrews crosses. I have a steel one now, but I think I'd like a wooden one as well. So I'll take one of those," he finished, dismissively motioning toward the Saint Andrew Cross in the corner.

"Any manacles or silk rope? Canes or floggers?" Brad offered helpfully.

The man shook his head and started toward the door. "No, I think I'm good for now. I'll pay for it today and send over one of my hired hands to pick it up Monday. I suppose that beautiful little slave in the cage doesn't go with it?"

Brad laughed heartily, handing him a slip of paper. "Afraid not. That's our shop helper. Eric is punishing her."

"Too bad. But I'm glad to see Eric wasn't completely destroyed by his last little sub. What was her name, Emily? That little girl, were she mine, would have been put over a bench and flogged until her ass had welts..."

Their voices drifted off as the door closed behind them. Luckily the room was warm so she wasn't cold. Though it seemed an eternity before the door opened again. Her knees hurt and her mind had gone numb. She'd almost fallen asleep a few times.

Eric crossed his arms over his chest. "It seems your lovely display sold a cage. It's been a little longer than two hours so I'm going to let you out."

She was afraid to meet his gaze so she kept her eyes downcast.

He walked across the room and opened the cage. "Get dressed; use the restroom if you have to. There's some lunch left over up front if you're hungry. It's only three o'clock. We still have a few hours before closing. Then I thought we'd go to Bistro Forty-One in Tiddsdale for dinner."

She nodded numbly. "Okay."

With that he left the room and she chastised herself. What the hell was she doing saying okay? Her *boss* had just stuck her *naked in a cage* for two-and-a-half hours! If she had any sense at all she'd just leave. There was nothing keeping her here. There were other jobs and she'd find something just as good. Then she remembered the paycheck. Her last few checks were better than what she'd gotten at her other jobs. Drawing in a deep breath she stood and put on her clothes as quickly as possible. Before going back into the front of the store she stopped off in the employee restroom and freshened up. Cautiously she stepped back into the store. She really hadn't decided what she was doing. She didn't want to leave just because she knew the *reality* of her prospects for as good a job weren't *that* good. At the same time, was it worth being caged? Well, it's not like they would do stuff like that *just because*, she assured herself. After all, she *had* broken the rules. She just wouldn't break any more rules and she wouldn't end up in a cage again. Besides, the cage was sold, unless they had another one boxed somewhere, waiting. Not to mention she liked it.

Brad was behind the computer again and Eric was at his usual place behind the register.

She had no idea what to say.

The store traffic had died down considerably and a few customers milled about flipping through books.

Brad was the first one to break the silence. "So eBooks."

"What about them?" Eric said with a frown.

"I was thinking we could consider selling eReaders." He shrugged and looked both of them expectantly.

Amy couldn't hide the surprised look on her face. Was that it? Would they never discuss her being naked in the cage again? Or was this so normal for them that it just wasn't a big deal?

"Why are you both looking at me like I have two heads?" Brad threw his hands up and leaned back in the chair.

"So let me get this straight," Eric looked at Amy as if he were speaking for both of them. "We sell eReaders and encourage people to buy eBooks that we don't sell?"

Amy couldn't help but nod in agreement. Eric had a point. "But you could put up a website and encourage local and indie authors, maybe a few small presses, to offer eBooks through your site, and just install WiFi here. Let people hook up, buy and download books from your website. Maybe put some café tables over there by the magazines and put a public computer terminal here on this side of the counter so that people can browse the catalog."

Brad gave her a broad smile. "That's visionary. Of course it could take a few months to put into place. What do you think, Eric?"

Eric frowned, clearly thinking about it. "Maybe we could try it. It also means we're going to need to find someone to design the website and get together with some small publishers and independent authors to discuss selling the books in a format the eReaders can read."

Brad continued to grin. "I'm just worried if we don't keep up with the new technology we're going to be left behind and end up out of business."

"Well, we could always open a public shop for the other merchandise if it came down to it." Eric suggested. He winked at Amy. And just like that, Amy felt excitement run through her at his warm regard toward her. Any anger she may have felt toward him for caging her vanished.

This time it was Brad's turn to frown. "And deal with the city council and hard core Christian groups? I'd rather stay under *that* radar. Though we could always use Amy as a floor model if we ever decided to go that route."

Eric shook his head and rolled his eyes. "We'd have nothing to punish her for. She's already broken the only rule we have and now it no longer applies since she already knows what's behind doors number one and two."

It was as if she wasn't even in the room.

"Well then I guess we'll have to make new rules. The guy comes in for a bench and a spreader bar," Brad lowered his voice when a customer came in. "And next thing I know he buys a cage and a cross. That's a lot of money and I'm pretty sure it's because he liked what he saw in the cage and she gave him a better *vision* of his home playroom."

Eric lifted an eyebrow as if he were considering it.

Amy finally found her voice. "Umm, I realize I broke the rule and I took my punishment without complaint, but if this is going to be a regular thing I'm not so sure I can…" Her voice trailed off as they both looked at her. She swallowed hard - again.

Eric's light brown eyes went from serious to amused almost instantaneously. "She has a point. She hasn't really consented to play."

"And yet you saw fit to punish her for sneaking around," Brad said in a subdued tone. There were still customers around, even though none of them were around the register.

"Well," Eric turned to her, "Next time we say you need to stay out of a particular room will you stay out of it?"

She nodded almost instinctively and murmured, "Yes, Sir."

He turned back to Brad, "There you go. Besides, she's a sub and everyone behind this counter knows it."

Brad nodded. "Well, you two work it out. Oh, and Amy – since you've already been in the back rooms you can go in there now, with authorization this time. Are we clear on that?"

"Yes, Sir," she told him.

"Go start cleaning up the shelves and getting them back in order. We're doing inventory tomorrow night and the shelves need to be as orderly as possible. It makes inventory a lot easier," Brad ordered.

She nodded, "Yes, Sir. Do you want me to work late tomorrow night?"

"Don't you have homework?" Eric asked in an almost scolding tone.

"Well, yeah, but," she started.

Eric cut her off. "No. You need to have time to get homework done."

Brad nodded in agreement. "I guess you better do your homework or you'll end up bent over one of those spanking benches with a flogger across your ass."

Her eyes went wide, her face red, and a strange smile crossed her face. She hurried off to the shelves to spend the rest of the afternoon straightening things up. When she got to the bdsm section she was tempted to flip through another book, but decided against it. There were a few older men nearby and a woman was browsing the horror novels just across from her. She didn't want to get caught looking, not to mention she didn't want Eric or Brad to come along and see that she was actually interested in learning more about it.

The idea of Eric spanking her actually caused a rush of excitement to flood through her and she felt herself dampen at the thought. What was wrong with her? Confusion and guilt coursed through her. She didn't know how to feel. She remained confounded until closing.

Once they'd closed the shop she found herself in Eric's car, heading toward dinner. Amy decided she couldn't just not talk about it or act like it didn't happen. It had been treated with such nonchalance at the bookstore that her head was still reeling. Confused, she looked at Eric who seemed wholly unconcerned.

"I really think we need to talk about the whole cage thing some more," she started carefully.

Eric lifted an eyebrow. "Okay."

"I need to know why, why I liked it and was so willing and why I'm so confused," she admitted.

He was quiet for a moment, and then said, "Understandable. You read all that fiction in one sitting, perhaps you should look into some non-fiction about the subject. Each sub has her own reason for being a sub. Some just get off on being dominated, others actually need the release submission provides, and then there's the pain aspect where a sub needs the sting of the whip or the smack of a hand in order to release emotionally. You might actually understand that," he said, nodding toward her arms. "In submission some people can relax or emotionally recover from stress or emotional pain. I'd say you're a combination of those types, many subs are," he told her.

She thought about this briefly then posed the challenge, "So what if I decide I want to stick you in a cage?"

He laughed. "Then we'd call you a switch. Switches can be Doms or subs depending on who they're with. Do you want to stick me in a cage?"

She rolled her eyes. Admittedly the thought of caging him did nothing for her. "No."

He chuckled. "It's understandable you're confused. I've met a lot of subs over the years. Brad and I had you picked out for one the day we met you. Sometimes a sub doesn't know she's a sub until she meets a Dom and experiences submission."

"Can't men be subs, too?"

"Oh, sure. I was using the general term *she* since you're a she. You remember Mistress Kali?"

How could she forget the dragon lady who wanted to use her as a test subject presumably for her new whips and bdsm furniture? She smiled and shook her head. "Yeah. How could I forget?"

Eric nodded. "She's the most sought after Domme in the state. All the Dommes wish they were her. If you ever want to experience a Domme topping you I could probably arrange it."

Amy jumped. "Oh no. I'm not going there. You better not hand me over to the dragon lady."

Laughing, Eric pulled into the restaurant parking lot and parked. "Okay, so that's one of your boundaries. I'll keep that in mind."

"Yet you never considered sticking me in a cage would be a boundary?"

"That was different. That was a punishment. Boundaries aside, you weren't supposed to go into the locked rooms without permission and you did. I could have very well taken a cane to your ass for that, but then I thought *that* would have crossed boundaries since we hadn't agreed to anything rough. The cage was probably a bit severe. I suppose I could have made you stand in a corner or something less humiliating. But then that may have not been enough to get the point across," he said thoughtfully.

They got out of the car and went into the restaurant. All the while Amy contemplated what he'd said. He had seriously considered it all.

Once seated, Eric leaned toward her. "Face it, Amy; you're clearly interested in a little more exploration. Maybe not as hands on. We could stop by the club later and have a drink."

"Like a bdsm club?" She could feel the terror run through her. She wasn't sure she was quite ready for that.

"Yes, but only as an observer and I'd keep you with me at all times and wouldn't let you out of my sight," he paused. "For education only, I promise."

She thought about a response before she answered. "Maybe. So you and your ex were both into the scene?"

He nodded and took a drink from the iced tea in front of him.

"So I overheard something about her and if I'm prying just tell me it's none of my business," she paused, remembering back to what the client from earlier had said to Brad. "She did something really bad to you, didn't she?"

Taking a deep breath he leaned toward her again. "I see you and Brad have been talking…"

"Actually I overheard the customer who bought the cage say something to Brad about her and you," she said. It wasn't a lie, but she didn't want him to know she had talked to Brad, too.

"Such as?" He sat back with a raised eyebrow.

"Well, I wasn't straining to listen, he said it right in front of me," she corrected, not liking the change in Eric's posture. "He said something about being glad you had moved on from your ex and if a sub ever did to him what your ex did to you that he would have beat her ass until there were welts."

His expression softened. "Yeah, well, after we'd agreed to an exclusive relationship unless we were having a ménage with other mutually agreed upon partners, she decided to start having an affair behind my back. She was living with me, not working, we were exclusive and not even doing public scenes, and she started cheating on me with some young guy at the club. Let's just say I found out about it almost immediately. I confronted her about it and she lied to my face, so I left the store early one afternoon and followed her straight to his place..." His voice trailed.

Amy didn't know what to say. "And?"

"I knocked on the door, I was told to come in, I did, and they were already screwing and expecting another guy to join them evidently, because he showed up a few minutes later."

"Wow. What a bitch!" Amy started to feel guilty for asking. "And you said only people my age had drama."

"Touché. Anyway, obviously she couldn't lie. I didn't want to start a fight so I just told her it was over and she had until the following weekend to get out, and she starts running after me telling me how much she loves me." He shrugged as if trying to act like it wasn't a big deal. "I was in love and blind."

"That really sucks. I'm sorry that happened to you. Some women can be bitches," Amy said quietly. Then she wondered if that's why Eric wanted to take her to the club. To show the ex that he'd moved on, too. "Does she still go to the club?"

Another deep sigh emerged from his chest. "Unfortunately, yes. But we keep our distance and have done a pretty good job ignoring each other for almost a year now. Maybe it's been a bit longer."

"Does she show up with guys just to flaunt them at you?"

He chuckled. "You women all belong to the same club or something?"

"What?"

"How did you know she did that?"

"Lucky guess. I have friends who'd do that sort of thing. So did you do the same?"

A short span of silence passed between them. "No. I haven't really been with anyone since."

"Not even dates?"

"Not really. One or two dinner dates but not to the club," he said in a subdued tone. "I kind of know what I'm looking for."

"Oh. Well maybe you *should* take me to the club then. You can show me off a little and I can satiate my curiosity. I bet I'm younger and prettier than she is," Amy gave him her most brilliant flirtatious smile.

He smiled back at her then said in a very sexy baritone, "That you are. Just don't get too big for your britches or I'll have to take you across my knee."

A rush of excitement ran through her. The thought of being draped over his knee and his hand smacking her ass made her tremble. Her panties were immediately moist. "Yeah, well, if I was in a relationship with a guy and we agreed it was exclusive, it would be. I'm ferociously loyal. Women like that give women a bad name," she said with some venom. She was feeling very protective toward him right now - as silly as that sounded. It only reinforced what she already knew. She liked Eric a lot and even her initial shock and chagrin at being caged nude wasn't enough to make her not want to be with him. Not to mention she had to admit that being caged really turned her on.

They ate and continued talking, taking the conversation back to books and movies and their favorite hiking and camping spots. Once they'd finished dinner and found themselves back in the car Eric turned to her. "So do you really want to go check out the club?"

She felt her chest tighten, but she wanted to go, if for no other reason to help Eric get back at his ex. "Yes, but only to observe and check it out, right?"

"Yes."

"Am I dressed appropriately?" she asked carefully, looking down at her nice jeans, the black V-neck blouse and a pretty pair of strappy black leather sandals with a wedge heel. She'd even given herself a pedicure and manicure with a deep maroon polish in anticipation of their date that wasn't really a date. Oh who was she kidding, it was a date.

He let out a laugh. "Personally I like short skirts, but yeah, for someone who isn't participating you're dressed fine."

Making a mental note that he liked short skirts she asked, "Any protocol I should observe?"

"I'm glad you asked," he said in a suddenly serious way. "Don't look anyone in the eye. It's bad form for a sub to look at a Dom. Also, don't talk to anyone unless I say it's okay. Stay with me at all times, and if anyone touches you or talks to you without my permission you need to let me know. That's not allowed."

"So possessiveness is encouraged?" That seemed really strange to her.

"Well, you have to remember that most people are there to play. For singles, it's fine because the subs and Doms both know what they're there for. But you just want to observe. So by pretending to be mine, you stave off Doms looking for subs and you also keep at bay people who want a play partner. There are also some inexperienced Doms who think any sub they talk to or who talks to them should immediately call them Sir or Master and bend to their will. But there are also dungeon monitors who are there for everyone's safety. If for any reason we get separated and you don't know what to do, find one of the guys wearing the red arm band and tell them you're with me and that we got separated and they'll get you back to me safe and sound."

She took in the information. "I am going to need a drink. Maybe a glass of wine."

"I'll make sure that's the first thing you get," he assured her.

They drove in silence, the anticipation building. It seemed to take forever. She noticed Eric glancing over at her every few minutes. When they pulled into the parking lot there were a few people milling about. "You really want to go in?"

Drawing in a deep breath she looked at the neon sign that announced to all that this place was called *The Black Lily*. "Yes," she whispered.

They got out of the car and she stepped up next to Eric, who took her hand into his. "Just hold my hand. You must be really freaked out, you're trembling."

"Just nervous," she admitted.

"Well, take a few deep breaths," he said, carefully leading her across the parking lot to the front door. There were two huge guys standing guard there.

"Eric!" the bald guy greeted. He looked Amy up and down. "Nice to see you back, man."

"You saw me earlier this week," Eric told him.

"No man," he nodded toward Amy. "Back."

"Yeah, thanks."

"Oh by the by, buddy, Emily's here," he called after them as they passed over the threshold into the darkness beyond.

Amy felt Eric's hand tighten around hers. "Ow," she whispered.

He loosened his grip and gently pulled her close to him as they made their way past the ticket window with a nod to the woman behind the glass, down a hallway, and into the club beyond. "Sorry, just tensed up," he whispered in her ear.

Amy's mind raced. So the ex, Emily, was there. She wondered if he'd point her out. It would be fucked up for her to ask so she didn't. Just then her thoughts subsided and she focused on what was going on around her. To say people dressed the part was an understatement. The forward part of the bar was just that, a bar. But a lot of women were dressed scantily and they even passed a man wearing nothing but a G-string. There were large round metal cages next to the walls. A few them were occupied by women wearing ball gags and with their hands bound behind their backs. A cold terror ran through her and she clutched at Eric.

He gave her hand a reassuring squeeze and they sat down at one of the tables. Leaning into her he whispered into her ear. "Don't worry. No one is going to do anything to you here." For a moment he pressed his lips into her hair and breathed in deeply.

She held his hand and kept her eyes downcast.

"What can I get for you, Sir?"

"A glass of Chardonnay for the lady and I'll have a Guinness. Thanks, Mel. Tell Brian to make the glass of wine a big one. Long day," Eric said. He took his hand from Amy's and draped his arm over her shoulders, pulling her to him.

Needing something to hang onto, she put her left hand on his thigh and her right hand on his chest.

"Be careful," he whispered.

"Why," she asked.

"I don't know how long I can handle being this close to you," he said in a low growl.

That's when she realized his cock was straining in his black jeans only a few inches from her hand. It was so tempting to slide her hand up to feel it through the thick fabric. She refrained, pressing her thighs together to stop the tingling sensation between them. Pulling away from him, she made herself comfortable on the bar table stool and leaned on the table.

Two men approached the table. She only glanced at them, didn't make eye contact, and looked at her hands.

"Hey Eric. You going into the back tonight?" the shorter man with black hair graying at the temples asked. He was wearing a red arm band.

Eric shrugged. "Don't know yet. Depends if Amy is feeling adventurous enough to check it out."

The taller guy with blond hair cropped short said, "First timer?"

She noticed he was wearing one of the red arm bands, too. She wondered why they weren't in the dungeon monitoring.

Eric nodded and ran his hand down her back. "Just checking things out. Relaxing after a long day."

"Well, we're on break, but maybe we'll see you guys in the back later." With that, both men moved through the crowd, past the bar into a door that said Employees Only.

"That was Peter and Lance, a few of the Dungeon monitors," he told her. Then he sucked air between his teeth. "And here comes Mistress Kali."

Amy made an audible gasp and threw a hand up to her mouth to cover it.

"Eric, darling!" She strode up wearing a pair of black latex pants, patent leather heels, and a latex top that again, gave her ample cleavage. "What is her name again?"

Eric smiled at her. "Amy."

"I thought she was just your shop girl, but now I see you just didn't want to share your sub," Kali said with a mock pout.

Just then the bar maid showed up with their drinks. Eric immediately handed the glass of wine to Amy. "It's okay to take a few big swigs of that," he told her, then turned to Kali. "Umm, yeah. So how are you?"

"I'm here with Alexa and Dan who are at the bar getting me a drink. Is Emily here tonight?" She lifted a manicured eyebrow with a coy smile.

"I heard she was, but I haven't seen her and I really don't care. Amy and I just stopped by for a drink and if she feels up to it, we might go take a seat in the back for a few minutes just so she can look around." Eric said simply.

Kali looked Amy and Eric up and down a few times and shook her head. "Well, we're not doing any scenes tonight, but we are going watch Master Robert and Amanda. They're doing a Shibari demonstration on stage four in half an hour."

Amy felt her eyes go wide. They scheduled demonstrations? She choked back a surprised laugh and took a gulp of the wine. Keeping her eyes downcast, she took a deep breath.

Continuing Kali said, "Definitely come back and sit at our table. We'll save two seats for you." Then she regarded Amy with a bright smile and leaned into Eric. She whispered something then she winked at him and headed toward the bar where a man and woman stood waiting for her.

Amy took another swig of the wine noticing Eric's expression seemed tenser than before. She'd insisted they come and now she was regretting it. "I'm sorry, maybe this wasn't a good idea."

"No," he protested. "Sorry, Kali just told me about something she overheard and it pissed me off. We really should go back and watch. Master Robert and his sub Amanda put on a great demonstration and Amanda always wears a bathing suit so... They don't do full nudity in their scenes."

"Oh," Amy said, taking another gulp of the wine and realizing she'd drained the glass. "I think that would be okay."

"Good." He took the empty wine glass and handed it to the bar maid who had magically appeared with another glass of wine. Then he set the full glass of wine in front of her. "Let's go sit now so we don't have to try to navigate a huge crowd."

Taking their drinks he led the way, Amy hurrying along behind him, hanging onto the back of his jeans.

The back of the club was dimly lit by a few wall sconces and small lamps that hung over the tables. At the edges of the room, inset into the walls, were stages, presumably where the demonstrations took place. She hung onto Eric's belt loop and followed him through the crowd, careful not to look anyone in the eye. She certainly didn't want to call attention to herself. Finally, Eric stopped at a table right in front of what looked to be the main stage. Sitting there was Mistress Kali and her entourage.

She gave Eric another flashy smile. It was obvious, by Amy's estimation, that Kali was interested in him and it put her stomach in knots. She didn't want to share Eric, especially with a woman like Kali. Eric pulled out a chair to the right for Amy and ushered her into it. He took the chair to her left, creating a barrier between her and Kali for which she was thankful. Then he rested his arm over her shoulders, looking around the room as if to ward off anyone who might have been looking at Amy in *that* way. She didn't say anything, just opened her senses to the cacophony of voices. It almost sounded like the buzzing of bees. She felt Eric squeeze her shoulder, causing a flood of sensation through her.

Eric leaned forward and whispered into her ear, "You can relax at any time, Amy. I promise I won't let anything happen to you."

Sucking in a deep breath she nodded and whispered back, "Okay."

Then Eric did something that sent shots of pleasure through her. He gently kissed her ear. Her nipples went hard and she let out a tiny gasp. He didn't remove his hand from her shoulder. Instead, he leaned back and starting chatting casually with Kali and her male escort about cars. Amy couldn't get into it. She was entirely too mesmerized by the club. The lights, the people, the stages. Eric's large hand protectively on her at all times.

"Two o'clock. I guess you're safe to approach now?" Kali said, nodding her head to the side.

Eric turned his head toward the direction Kali indicated and audibly groaned, "Great."

Amy couldn't help but give him a questioning look.

She didn't have to wait long to find out what was up because Kali said in a mocking tone, "Emily, dear, how brave of you to approach a table of Doms when you are most certainly not welcome."

"I apologize for intruding, Mistress. I was only hoping to speak with Master Eric," came a soft voice from behind Amy.

Amy resisted the temptation to turn and look at the intruder. Emily. The ex-girlfriend.

"You and I have nothing to discuss, Emily," Eric said in a flat, cool voice.

But she persisted. "Can we speak in private, Master Eric? Just for a few minutes?"

Amy felt eyes on her, but she still didn't dare turn around. Being at the club was awkward enough. She hadn't actually expected Eric's ex-girlfriend would approach them.

Kali seemed to notice this. She didn't hold back how she really felt. "Well Eric, you might as well. I'll keep your current girlfriend occupied while you deal with the ex."

"I'm sorry about this. I'll be right back," he said.

Amy slowly turned her head to see Eric leave the table, the scrawny brunette dressed in a latex mini leading the way. She completely dropped the protocol. "What the hell was that?"

Letting out a laugh, Kali leaned toward her. "Now that she sees you have him, she wants him back. That's what *that* is. Despite all this," she motioned toward the room around them, "that little girl had Eric wrapped around her little finger from day one. She's a manipulative beast and were she mine..."

"You would have put her over a spanking bench and given her a good flogging until her ass had welts?" Amy finished.

Laughter resounded around the table.

"That and more, perhaps something more severe," Kali said with a wink.

Amy felt herself blush a little and she took a gulp of her wine.

"And who is this enchanting creature?" a male voice boomed from behind her.

"That's Eric's sub, Amy, and he won't share, so don't ask," Kali said flatly. "So how are you today, Thomas?"

Thomas answered, "Fine," and then he and Kali's voices went distant. Amy no longer heard them. She wanted Eric to come back. Was Emily begging him to take her back? What could that woman possibly want with him? They were over - they had been for over a year according to Eric. Eric promised not to leave her and yet he had, even though Mistress Kali was proving to be a good deterrent to any Doms looking at Amy as if she were fresh meat.

"What did I miss?" Amy look up so quickly something pulled in her neck. It wasn't Eric standing there; it was Brad who had replaced the Dom named Thomas. For some reason it seemed really strange seeing him here even though she knew he was involved with the club, too.

"We're waiting for the Shibari demonstration and Eric is dealing with Emily," Kali told him and gave Amy another wink.

Brad took Eric's chair and sat down. "You alright?" he asked Amy.

She nodded. "I'm fine. I've got wine."

With a laugh he leaned over to Kali and asked her something.

Kali shrugged. "I don't know, probably begging him to take her back. Fascinating how she only saw fit to do that the first time she catches Eric with someone else. She's a skanky bitch."

He asked her something else.

Kali shook her head then asked Amy, "She didn't say anything to you, did she?"

Amy shook her head. "Nope."

"Well here he comes, I guess we'll find out?" Brad said.

Eric let out a sigh and shook his head as he approached the table. Instead of asking Brad to move he took the chair on Amy's right. "Sorry about that," he told her.

She shrugged, not wanting to let him know how much she hated that he'd left her to go talk to his ex. But she wasn't going to hold it against him. It was what it was and he likely would have had to deal with Emily sooner or later. That was the thing with ex's. Especially if things were left unresolved. She mused that she'd probably have to deal with her own ex-drama eventually. She shoved the thought of Paul out of her mind.

"So what did the bitch want?" Kali asked. She was certainly blunt.

"Wanted me to give her another chance," Eric said with a clenched jaw. "I explained to her that the only reason she wanted another chance was because I was with another woman and had moved on and she couldn't deal with that."

"And?" Brad asked.

"Then I told her no, that I was with someone else, and I suggested she move on, too. Though honestly I thought she had since she's been here every other week with a new guy." A sly smile crossed his lips.

Brad and Kali laughed. Amy didn't.

Eric took her hands into his and caught her gaze. "Don't worry, I'm totally over her."

Smiling Amy said, "I know." Though she wasn't completely sure. "Where's the ladies room?"

Kali jumped up. "I'll go with you."

Eric lifted an eyebrow.

"What? I already know she's off limits and I'll keep all the Doms off of her." With a flourish, Kali stepped around the chairs and headed toward the toilets, Amy right behind her.

Looking into the mirror with the garish overhead fluorescents, Amy thought she looked a bit exhausted. She re-applied some face powder and fixed her hair and lip gloss. She was so involved in wanting to look good for Eric she didn't notice the small brunette come up behind her, trailed by an equally petite redhead.

"So you're the woman who thinks she's going to take Eric from me?" the brunette asked.

Amy turned around, realizing Kali was probably still in one of the stalls. She figured she should probably point out the obvious. "Umm, I didn't know you were part of the equation in me and Eric's relationship until tonight. Besides, I heard you stepped out on him so if you don't have him anymore it's your own fault."

Emily took a step toward her. "I don't think you understand me. You need to step off. I don't want to see you here with him again."

A surge of anger ran through her. "I don't think you have any say in the matter. Maybe *you're* the one who needs to step off."

"How old are you? Like barely twenty-one?" the redhead chimed in.

"Why, jealous?" Amy smirked.

That's when Emily's small fist connected with Amy's jaw. It didn't hurt at first. Not until she regained her bearings did it begin to sting. "I can't believe you just hit me. Seriously bitch?"

Amy realized then that Kali had emerged from one of the stalls and was watching in disbelief. "As an off duty dungeon monitor I'm obligated to report this incident to the management. You do realize what this means, Emily?"

"She started it." Emily was visibly nervous.

"I was here the whole time and I heard every word. She didn't start anything. *You* started it." Kali started toward the door.

"Mistress Kali, no, wait, please..." Emily started.

Kali ignored Emily and stood half in and half out of the ladies room door. "I've got an unruly sub in here who hit another one," she was saying to someone just outside the door.

Emily turned toward Amy and took a step forward. "This is all your fault."

Amy took a step back, not believing the audacity of the woman. "Maybe you need to learn to take responsibility for yourself. This is no more my fault than it is that Eric no longer wants to have anything to do with you," Amy said, cupping her jaw with her right hand. Great, now she was going to have a bruise. That was going to be fun explaining to her uptight parents. She could hear the conversation now.

With a wave of her hand, Kali motioned Emily toward the door. "Master Bruce will escort you into the admin office and they'll decide if your club days are over, or if you're put on probation."

With one backward glare at Amy, Emily and her red-headed friend stomped out of the restroom leaving Amy and Kali looking at each other. "Get me an ice compress, I'll take care of Amy," Kali told whomever was outside the door.

Amy looked into the mirror. It was only a little red and the sting was slight.

Kali came up next to her and took her chin in her hand, tipping her head to where she could see her jaw and cheek better. "You may get lucky and it might not bruise, but a cold compress all the same. I can't believe that girl actually hit you."

Amy nodded. Maybe Kali wasn't so bad after all. Just a bit eccentric. "My luck I'd go out on a date with a guy who has a psycho ex."

"I wouldn't necessarily call her psycho, just very damaged," Kali said.

There was a knock on the restroom door. With a flourish, Kali answered it, retrieving an ice pack from the male hand belonging to whoever was out there. She brought it over to Amy. "Put this on your jaw."

Amy looked at herself in the mirror again. She was going to have to fix her makeup – again. She noticed Kali regarding her.

"So how do you like working at the bookstore?"

"I love it. It's a lot of fun actually," Amy said, noticing it ached when she made the long 'e' sound. "Eric and Brad are fun bosses. Unless you don't do what you're told."

Kali laughed and lifted the ice pack off her cheek and inspected the area. "I think you're lucky that Emily hits like a girl."

Amy laughed. "Yeah, maybe a little powder and no one will notice."

"You really like Eric?" the Domme asked with a raised eyebrow.

"Eric is great. We've gotten along really well since day one. I'm still a bit wary about all of this, but he says I'm a sub." She shrugged.

"Honey, do you get excited being told what to do and does the thought of him bending you over his knee to spank you get you hot? Or maybe him tying you up and having his way with you? Maybe the idea of a cane across your ass titillates you?" Kali gave her a quick smirk and opened Amy's bag, pulling out the powder compact. She began dabbing powder on the injured area.

Blushing, Amy said, "Well, yeah, I guess."

"Then you're definitely a sub and that's why Eric is into you. Eric is one of those guys who doesn't date casually if you know what I mean. He could top half the subs in this bar with the snap of his fingers if he wanted them. Instead, he goes for the brainy girls that stimulate and interest him not only sexually, but intellectually. Evidently you got both going for you, darlin'. And right now there are about fifty women in this place who hate you."

She couldn't hide the mortification she felt. "You mean more women are going to attack me?"

A bright laugh escaped Kali's red painted lips. "No, dear. Most subs will have the sense to hate you from afar, seething with jealousy. So have you and Eric ever?"

Amy's mouth dropped open. "No! This is our first date. I've only known him for three weeks."

"But he's told you what to do and you've done it?" Kali pressed.

"He's my boss, of course."

"Not exactly what I meant, but that will do. So what have you done? You can tell me. If you don't, Brad will."

"Well that's not fair," Amy started. "If I tell you do you promise not to breathe a word?"

"Spill it girlie! Chin up!" She dabbed more powder on Amy's cheek.

"I broke a rule at the store and I was punished."

Kali's eyes lit up. "A rough spanking?"

"Not exactly."

The Domme put the powder compact back into Amy's purse and handed it back to her. "He tied you up?"

Amy blushed. "No."

"Whips?" Kali suggested, this time with a look of excitement.

"Nothing that extreme," Amy said, her face flushing.

"Well out with it," Kali whispered.

"He put me in a cage." Amy shrugged as if it was no big thing.

A wide grin slid over Kali's lips. "Clothes on or off?"

"Off."

"He is a wicked little boy! I have to tell you, I lust after Eric completely, but all in good fun and fantasy. The problem is he won't switch sides. I'm a Domme, he's a Dom. Plus, I don't think I'm his type, but it's fun to ask him. I love that look he gets when he thinks I want to tie him up. It's priceless. We just won't tell him or Brad about our little conversation, no?" Kali gave her an expectant grin.

Amy shook her head. "Not a word."

"I suppose we should turn the protocol back on. You okay?"

"Yes, Mistress," Amy said with a shy smile.

Kali grabbed the ice pack and ushered Amy out the door. In the hallway one of the dungeon monitors stood guard.

"Is everything alright Mistress Kali?" he asked.

Kali handed him the ice pack. "Yes, thank you. She's fine. I'll take her back to Master Eric."

Next thing Amy knew she was sitting back between Eric and Brad watching in fascination as the man on stage artfully wound the rope around his female partner, binding her in such a way that her sex was exposed even though she was wearing a leotard. Amy imagined herself in the woman's position. Even clothed it would be humiliating to be bound like that. She imagined Eric binding her, being able to touch every inch of her flesh. She wondered what it would feel like to have rope binding her breasts. Her breath quickened and her heart pounded. Eric's hand rested gently on her knee and squeezed. That's when she realized he was watching her reaction with a great deal of pleasure.

He leaned into her and whispered gently in her ear, "You want to come home with me tonight and let me tie you up?"

Amy almost came right there. More than anything she wanted to go home with him. But she was afraid. She bit her lip. "Maybe," she whispered back.

With a sly grin he squeezed her leg and moved his hand further up her thigh. "You torture me."

They finished watching the demonstration, all the while Eric watching her and caressing her hand and thigh.

He leaned into her again. "So?"

She took a deep breath and decided in that second to make a huge leap. "You're the Dom, you tell me."

She almost regretted it the second she said it because something switched on in Eric. She saw it flicker in his eyes. It was controlled, calculated lust. It was dominance. She shuddered realizing she had just agreed to give control over to him. It was exciting.

"I think it's time to go. Get up," he ordered. He turned to the rest of the table. "I think Amy and I are leaving."

Kali gave her a private smile and with that, Eric took her by the hand and led her out of the club.

He opened the door and helped her into the car, then got into the driver side. Once they had pulled out of the parking lot onto the main street he asked, "So what took you and Kali so long in the bathroom?"

"Oh, umm..." she wasn't sure she should tell him, it could ruin the whole night.

"I asked you a question, Amy. Answer it and address me as Sir," he told her. "We'll work our way to Master."

Fear and excitement pulsed through her. "Yes, Sir." She took a deep breath. "I ran into your ex-girlfriend in the restroom and she punched me in the face."

The car swerved to the side of the road and he threw it in park. He turned to her, red with anger. "That bitch hit you?"

"Eric, I'm fine. Really. Kali took care of it."

He blinked and let out the breath he'd been holding. "I'm sorry. I didn't mean to lose control like that. How did Kali take care of it?"

"She handed her over to one of the dungeon monitors and said something about her future club involvement was in question or something like that," Amy said quietly. "Besides, Emily hit like a girl. It was barely a bump, we put some ice on it, threw some makeup over it and it's gone. See?" She lifted her chin and pointed to her jawline where the blow struck.

He turned on the overhead lamp in the car and looked at her face, gently caressing her cheek. "Okay. Stay here for a minute."

With that he got out of the car. Amy watched him go to the back of the car and lean against it, his cell phone poised over his ear. He talked to someone for a few minutes but she couldn't hear what was said. Then he got back into the car and carefully pulled back into traffic.

"I'm sorry I lost my temper, it's just that Emily had my dander up already."

Amy stifled a giggle.

"What?"

"Well, Sir, I thought only my dad used words like *dander*." She laughed again.

"Ah, old jokes." He shook his head. "*That* deserves a spanking."

The thought of a spanking caused her to pull her thighs together tightly. She was so wet. It amazed her how he could sexually arouse her with just a sentence. "Yes, Sir."

Chapter Six

It didn't take long for them to arrive at Eric's house. It wasn't a small house either. It was a two story house with a three car garage, a big yard and a long driveway. Unfortunately parked in his driveway was a small gray hatchback with a woman leaning against the bumper, her hands crossed over her non-existent chest. It was Emily.

"Are you kidding me?" Eric said aloud as he pulled up next to Emily's car in the driveway. "Amy, stay in the car. I'll deal with this." He mumbled some unflattering curse words under his breath and got out.

"What the hell are you doing here?" Eric asked.

"That woman you're with got me kicked out of the club tonight. She pulled my hair so I hit her so she'd let go and then she convinced Mistress Kali that she was the victim. Thought you should know that she's a manipulative bitch."

"Yes, I know you don't like my girlfriend. I also know you don't like Kali. But I trust both of them tremendously more than I trust you. So again, what are you doing here?" Eric looked angry, but he stayed calm, controlled.

"Eric, I love you. Please give me a second chance. I made a mistake. We all make mistakes," she started.

"No." He said simply. "I've moved on from that. I don't think you understand not only how much you hurt me but I can never trust you again. It wasn't the first time you cheated, Emily."

Emily looked down at her feet. "I promise I've changed."

"You don't understand. Maybe you have changed, but so have I. I've moved on. I no longer love you. I no longer want you. Please leave and if you harass Amy again, or attack her, we're pressing charges." He pointed to her car. "Now get back in your car and get off my property. You're not welcome here and if you don't leave I'll call the police and have you removed."

Emily let out an audible gasp. The shocked look on her face made Amy smile inwardly, but she kept a serious, cool expression on her face and didn't even flinch when Emily shot her a jagged glare through the car window. With excessive speed, she backed out of the driveway and her car disappeared down the street.

Once Eric seemed sure Emily was gone, he went to the passenger door and opened it for Amy. "She's gone. Hopefully for good this time." He didn't sound convinced.

Amy got out. She didn't know what to say, if anything. She wondered then if the universe was trying to tell her something. Maybe she and Eric weren't meant to be.

He locked the car and set the car alarm with a click of a button and started toward the front door. "Coming?"

She followed; speechless at how big the house was and how well kept the yard looked. Eric struck her as the rogue type. The kind of guy who lived in an apartment or a loft or something. Not a big house in a fancy suburb.

He unlocked the door then turned to look at her. Catching her gaze, like he always did, he said, "Let's not let her ruin our night. I seem to recall a comment about me being old for using a word... what was it?"

A smile spread across her face and she let out a laugh. "Dander."

He laughed. "I may have to regain my composure for a spanking, but you're due for one. But first, maybe a cup of coffee?"

She followed him into the entryway, surprised by the high ceilings. "Wow." Every bit of protocol was forgotten. "You live here all by yourself?"

He nodded. "I was under the crazy notion, once upon a time, that I'd get married and have kids."

Her heart caught in her chest. Oh God. That's what everyone meant when they said Emily had really given Eric the shaft. He had loved her enough that he had planned on marrying her. And now, Amy was probably the first woman who had been inside the house since Emily. "It could still happen," Amy said absentmindedly.

"Yeah, maybe someday," Eric agreed. "Kitchen is back this way."

The entire place was impeccably decorated and clean. "You're tidy and you have great decorating taste."

He laughed. "Well, I'm afraid you'll have to save your kudos for my sister because she's an interior decorator and I hired her to do my place. I also can't take credit for the cleanliness. I have a cleaning service come in weekly."

"Books must make good money."

"Wrong again. Good investment choices make a substantial amount of money. The bookstore is just something Brad and I enjoy. Don't get me wrong," he started with a shrug. "We aren't operating in the red. We turn a small profit with *By The Book*, but it's nothing compared to my investments. This house is already bought and paid for."

"Do you even live here?"

"Busted again," he laughed. "Mostly to eat, sleep, shower, shave and I sometimes have friends over."

"Does Brad live around here, too?" She looked into the dining room and saw a beautiful oak dinette with a huge china cabinet. The furnishings alone looked seriously expensive.

"About four blocks from here actually. So coffee?"

"Yes, please." She followed him into the kitchen and sat on a stool at the breakfast bar. She couldn't help but look around. "I don't think I've ever been in a house this big."

"It sometimes gets a bit lonely, that's for sure." He started making coffee. "That's why I'm out most of the time."

She watched him make the coffee. He looked a little sad.

"Eric, I think we need to talk about Emily," she said.

He shook his head. "I don't have anything to say about Emily. I loved her, she didn't love me, but I was so in love with her that I was blind to her indifference."

Amy wondered then what kind of person could do that to someone else. Have a sexual relationship and live with a man without loving him, all so she had a place to stay, clothes on her back, and food on the table. Eric was quite a catch and any woman who threw that away was missing out.

"Uh oh. Deep thought?" He pushed the start button on the coffee pot.

"Just wondering what motivates a woman like Emily to treat a decent guy like you, like shit. I mean – with you she had everything."

"Brad thinks it's because I'm too nice and nice guys always finish last. I think it's because Emily had issues." He took a drink.

Amy raised an eyebrow. Kali had made a comment about Emily being damaged. "What kind of issues though? I mean daddy issues? Hell, I have daddy issues. My dad was disappointed I was born female and we don't talk much." She shrugged. It was just another one of those things about her life she'd grown to accept.

"Well I imagine we all have some issue with how we were raised. My own parents were very absent so I've always been closer to my friends than my family. Well, except my sister. I only see her five or six times a year though." He sat back and said thoughtfully, "In Emily's case it goes beyond absent parents. Her father was an abusive drunk. Her mother was a battered housewife. And the only non-violent attention Emily ever got from a male where she wasn't being smacked around was when she was molested by an uncle when she was thirteen. Somehow she got it in her head that if a man doesn't want her sexually, she's worth nothing to him. She also equates sex with love. So if any guy wants to have sex with her, she immediately thinks he loves her and she wants that. It's like it's programmed into her. Her entire self-identity and sense of self-worth is wrapped up in her sexuality. I was trying to help her work through that along with her therapist, but clearly it didn't work."

Amy bit her lip thoughtfully. In that moment she felt a great deal of pity for Eric's ex. "That sucks."

"Yeah." The coffee maker beeped and he grabbed two cups out of the cupboard. "But really, enough about that. I need to move forward with my life and I really don't want *her* to ruin our evening."

"I'm sorry I brought it up, I just thought maybe you'd feel better if you talked about it," she admitted, feeling a pang of guilt.

"Nah, it's okay. Have a look around if you want. Just don't try to get into any locked rooms."

From where she sat she could see into a family room. There was a big screen TV in there. She gave him a wry smile and ventured from the kitchen into the family room. From there she saw the sliding glass doors leading to a large deck. Beyond that there was an outdoor pool and a small building that looked like…

"Hot tub is out in the small building out there," he said coming up behind her. He ran his hands over her shoulders.

She turned to him, "So how do I get upstairs?"

He grinned. Their faces were mere inches apart. "Back to the main entry, take a left, then a right."

"Give me a tour," she said playfully.

"Fair enough." Taking her by the hand he led her to the staircase, but not before she noticed they were passing other rooms. "What are all the rooms down here?"

"Study-slash-library and the room with the pool table and video game systems in it. I guess you could call it the game room." He continued up the stairs.

She hurried after him. After looking over the huge main bathroom and guest rooms, he showed her the master suite. It was four times the size of her room at home and had a walk in closet and three piece bath. Shaking her head she just knew she was out of her league here.

"Come on. Back down for coffee. Besides, we didn't get to see my favorite room."

"There's more?" she asked.

"Yeah. Come on."

She followed him back downstairs and they had a cup of coffee while he told her how after he and Emily split, his sister had used his house to build her resume when she got out of school. "She had a professional photographer come in and take pictures and everything for her portfolio," he said.

"Did she get more jobs from it?"

Eric nodded. "Some big ones in this neighborhood actually, and a few others across town. She has her own business. Makes pretty decent money, too. It's something she can do even with the kids."

Smiling she said, "You have nieces and nephews?"

"One nephew, two nieces," he corrected.

"You didn't strike me as an uncle or a guy who owned a house," she admitted.

"Ah, so I was…?"

"The single rebel, estranged from his family who lived in a loft," she admitted.

He began laughing. "That's funny."

She felt her cheeks turn red. "You must think I'm some stupid naïve schoolgirl and you'd be right."

"No. I don't think that at all. Come here." He patted his lap.

She gave him a wary look.

"Serious, come here. I'm not going to put you over my knee yet, I promise."

Nervously she got up and went over to him, sitting on his lap with a sigh. He put his arms around her and rested his chin on her shoulder. "For the rest of the night I want you completely in the moment. I don't want you to worry about anyone or anything. I want you to relax and just let me take care of everything. Can you do that for me?"

A nervous flutter started in the pit of her stomach. "Yes, Sir."

His lips found her neck and he gently kissed her. A rush of warmth flooded her and her panties felt wet. She couldn't close her legs together though, not the way she was positioned. She felt exposed. Horny and exposed. His hands moved to her hips as he kissed up her neck moving upward to kiss her lips. She opened her mouth letting his tongue find its way into her, plunging deeply, entwining with hers. She kissed him back, deeply, passionately, every pore in her body aching for his exploration.

His lips and tongue found their way down her neck again and she arched her back, her breasts shoving toward him. She wanted him to touch them, caress them and lick them, but he didn't. His hands moved to her thighs and gently caressed them but never ventured any higher than mid-thigh. She gasped and thought any moment she would beg him to touch her. Then suddenly his exploration stopped.

"Stand up and take off all your clothes."

The order took her by surprise. She bit her lip and looked around.

"Take off your clothes," he repeated in a firm tone.

She took of her shoes and stockings first, then slowly slipped off her shirt. Then she removed her bra, letting it fall to the floor. His gaze watched her every move with a quiet anticipation and appreciation. She wiggled out of her jeans, letting them fall to the floor. Finally, she slid her panties off her hips and down to her ankles and gingerly stepped out of them. His eyes lingered between her legs and he licked his lips and looked up at her. She wanted to cover herself but knew he didn't want her to.

"Now, hands behind your back and legs spread so I can see you better."

She did as instructed.

He got up and walked around her, closely inspecting her pussy without touching her. She felt herself flush red. Then he moved behind her and took both her wrists into one hand, restraining her. He gently prodded her forward, "We're going to go down to the playroom for a while," he whispered in a voice that sounded almost like a primal growl.

She let him lead her through the family room to a staircase that led to a finished basement filled with equipment like the stuff she'd seen in the back room at the bookstore, including a cage. Her nipples were hard, her entire body tingling. When he stopped and wrapped soft restraint bands around her wrists she didn't protest. Instead, she simply closed her eyes and let him. The feeling of being bound and under his control made her feel safe. It also turned her on. She felt wetness drip from her pussy.

"Now I'm going to bathe you. Come on," he said in that same calm, domineering tone he'd used in the club when he told her they were leaving.

Again, she didn't argue and simply allowed him to lead her to the shower. After adjusting the temperature he took down the shower massage and ran it over her shoulders and breasts, down her stomach and between her thighs. Not once did he touch her, but instead allowed the water to caress and clean her soft, delicate skin. When he seemed satisfied she was clean he gently dabbed her dry with a towel. The towel between her legs made her whimper, but only because she wanted him to touch her. She yearned for it and even pushed her pelvis forward in hopes he'd at least know she wanted him.

"Not yet. Patience, beautiful," he cooed at her. Leading her to an exam looking table he undid her wrists from behind her back and took them over her head. "Keep your arms above your head and lay on the table."

She did as she was told, leaning back on the cold vinyl. Once in position he bound her hands above her head and put her feet in the stirrups of the exam table, using soft cuffs to bind her there and another set to pull her knees apart, spreading her sex before him.

She felt exposed and vulnerable. He could see every inch of her. The anticipation of not knowing what he was going to do excited her in ways she never imagined.

He ran his tongue down her inner thigh. She gasped and cried out, noticing he was watching her, pleased by her reaction. His tongue moved closer to her labia. Instinctively she tried to close her legs, but the restraints wouldn't allow it.

When his tongue slid skillfully over her pussy lips she jumped and cried out again, shoving her hips forward.

He moved back to her inner thighs, ignoring her pussy altogether. She couldn't stand it.

"It's time for a protocol lesson," he said, pulling back completely. "When there is something that scares you or hurts too much and you want to stop, you say red. Is that clear?"

"Yes, Sir," she answered, still breathless.

"What do you say?"

"Red, Sir."

"Good. Now where should I put my tongue?" He looked down at her body as if it was a plate of chocolates and he was choosing a piece. "I think I'll nibble on your stomach."

He kissed her stomach and licked it gently, looking up at her breasts knowingly. He knew she wanted him to suck on her breasts and clit and he wasn't going to and she knew it. He seemed to be having too much fun torturing her. She spent the next few minutes squirming beneath him, trying to draw attention to the areas where she wanted his attention with no success. Finally he smiled down at her and laughed. "If you want something, my little sub, you may ask for it."

She whimpered as his hand ran the length of her inner thigh and stopped short of her pussy. She couldn't ask him or tell him how she wanted to be touched. It was too embarrassing. Humiliating even. His hands ran over her stomach, along her sides, barely grazing the sides of her breasts. Her nipples went hard. She felt her pussy dripping with lust.

"Please Sir, touch my breasts," she cried out in a pitiful voice.

He growled. "Very good," he praised. With that his hands gently moved to her breasts and he lightly caressed them and ran a forefinger around each nipple slowly and carefully. She writhed in ecstasy, wanting his tongue on her breasts. As if he read her mind his mouth closed around a nipple and he sucked it roughly then moved to the other one and did the same thing. With his thumb and forefinger he squeezed her nipples and pulled slightly, causing her to cry out in pain. While it hurt, it sent a pleasing sensation through her wet sex and she shoved her hips upward.

"Please Sir, touch my pussy."

He chuckled, his hips only inches from her, the evidence of his arousal straining against the fabric of his pants. She could see the outline of his big cock and she wanted it between her legs.

He followed her gaze. "Oh no. You're not getting that. Not yet. Maybe not at all. I haven't decided yet. I don't know if I want to give you full pussy attention tonight." With that he pulled apart her labia and exposed her clit and the dripping wet hole below it and looked at her long and hard.

She knew he did it because it made her visibly uncomfortable. Not being able to stand it any longer she cried out in pure desperation, "Please, Master, please finger fuck me and suck my clit. Please."

A pleased look of surprise passed over his face. "Well now I don't think I can deny that. From Sir to Master in less than ten minutes, impressive." Slowly, he positioned himself between her legs, gently grazing her labia with his tongue. Then he dipped his tongue into her wet, wanting hole, pulled it out and slid it up to her swollen clit, circling it.

Moaning, Amy shoved her hips forward. He paused long enough to insert two fingers into her pussy, and then put his tongue back on her clit, working it in tight circles. His fingers moved inside her as if searching for something. When they hit the spot, she jumped and moaned and he continued rubbing that spot until her mind went numb with desire and pleasure.

She'd masturbated with a dildo but it didn't feel this good and neither of the men she'd been with ever did anything like this. His fingers moved expertly inside her and his tongue worked her clit. Restrained, she was helpless to stop him. Before she knew it, she was coming and her body spasmed and shuddered, bucking against him. She didn't want him to stop, but he did.

"Enough of that for now. Did you like that?"

She nodded, still gasping. "Yes Master."

"Mmm, I like the sound of Master. Good girl. Now there's the matter of your spanking for being insolent in the car earlier," he said.

She moaned, knowing she was going to be restrained and spanked and there was nothing she could do to stop him. *Except say red*, her mind reminded her. But she wouldn't. She wanted him to spank her. She'd been imagining it, wanting it, anticipating it. He removed the restraints tethering her to the table and helped her down, and then he took her to a spanking bench and bent her over it, re-tethering her wrists and ankles to the bench so she couldn't move. Her ass was in the air, exposed. He ran his hand over her ass cheeks.

"Ten good swats should do it, I think," he said. With that his palm came down on her left ass cheek with a loud smack. He alternated smacks on each cheek, each swat more painful than the last until finally, he reached ten and her ass stung. Then he softly caressed her.

Amy relaxed against the restraints and didn't move a muscle. That is until he pulled apart her ass cheeks and pushed a finger into her tight hole. She jumped and yelped at the sharp pain and clenched the hole closed.

He pulled his finger out. "I see we've found something my sweet little sub is uncomfortable with. We'll work on that."

Removing the restraints from her wrists and ankles he helped her up. Her entire body was tense and she realized she was shaking. He pulled her into his arms, gently rubbing her back and shoulders. "Relax my little sub. How about we put you in the cage for a while so you can rest."

He didn't wait for her to answer. He swung the cage door open and firmly pushed her in. She didn't protest. Instead, she climbed into the cage and curled up on the soft bedding lining the floor of it. He closed the door, watched her for a few minutes, and then went upstairs.

Amy was able to slow her breathing and relax a little. She looked around the room. It didn't look scary. Not how she imagined a real dungeon would look, and it was warm. Not to mention Eric had made this cage more comfortable, probably because she wasn't being punished. If he wanted to punish her all he had to do was remove the bedding. She closed her eyes.

She didn't know how long she'd been sleeping. Bleary eyed she sat up halfway, realizing she was still in the cage. She thought she heard voices from above, beyond the door, then she heard music and it dawned on her the noise was coming from the television.

The door opened and Eric descended the stairs, clearly noticing she was awake. His face was emotionless. She didn't like that. It made her uncomfortable not knowing what he was going to say or do. She craved his approval, or even that lustful look in his eye. The warmth of his smile.

Wiping some sleep from his eyes he leaned against the wall and looked at her as if deciding what to do with her. "You do look sexy in a cage," he finally said with a smile. "So the question is do we call it a night or do we play some more... I haven't decided."

She gulped, noting he hadn't asked her a question or offered her any input. Thirsty, she leaned against the bars of the cage helpless to his whims.

Like always, Eric seemed to notice her discomfort and disappeared around the corner to a part of the room Amy hadn't seen yet, returning with a paper cup with water in it. He handed it to her through the bars.

Taking it greedily, she drank deeply, feeling the cold wetness slide down her throat. Eric held out his hand, taking the cup from her and throwing it into a trash can that seemed to blend into the gray wall.

"Lie on your back and pull your knees to your chest," he finally ordered.

Doing as instructed she felt her face flush because the position exposed her fully for him. Eric came back around the cage with a dildo on a rod and pushed it through the bars and into her still moist hole. She whimpered.

"Don't move," he instructed. His forearm flexed as he worked the dildo in and out of her in long, slow strokes, pulling the head all the way out, then plunging it all the way in. Her clit began to ache and swell, but he didn't give her the attention she craved, instead he took his time, teasing her to where she almost couldn't stand it anymore.

She cried out in frustration. Why wouldn't he just pull her out of the cage already? She thought about asking and wondered if she should chance it. "Master, please let me out of the cage."

He narrowed his eyes. "Why?"

"I want to please you," she whispered, gasping slightly as the dildo filled her again.

"Ah, but I am content to watch you helpless in the cage taking every inch of this rubber cock into your tight pussy as it pleases me." He laughed slightly and shook his head. "How very manipulative of you, Amy. And very bad."

He pulled the pole and dildo from the cage and carefully put them in the utility sink. Walking back over to the cage he rubbed his hands together, again wearing a look that suggested he was debating what to do with her. With a lifted eyebrow he went over to the wall of whips and took down a flogger. From the corner he produced what Amy had learned was called a spreader bar. Tucking the whip in the waistband of his black pants he took a few other items she couldn't see and situated all the acquired items next to a bench, the approached the cage.

The cage door swung open. "Get out," he ordered.

She crawled out of the cage and stood up.

"Turn around, hands behind your back," he said in that same detached tone.

Doing as instructed, she felt him tug at the leather cuffs around her wrists and attach them together.

He pulled her wrists apart as if checking to make sure she couldn't get free. Then with a gentle yet firm grasp his large hand closed over her upper arm and he directed her to the bench. Eric's hand loosened its grip and he reached over and grabbed the spreader bar, pushing her feet apart and attaching the bar to her ankles.

She understood now why it was called a spreader bar; she couldn't close her legs even if she tried. Taking a deep breath she waited anxiously, wondering what Eric would do next. It wasn't a long wait.

"Open your mouth."

Opening her mouth to ask why, she found it immediately filled with a ball gag which he secured carefully behind her head.

He came around to the front of her so he could speak to her directly. "Since you can't speak and can't use a safe word, we're going to talk about using some signs to indicate everything's okay, or to stop. Do you understand?"

She nodded.

"To indicate you're okay, I want you to make the okay sign like this." He held up his hand, showing her. "For stop, two fingers like this. Do you understand?"

She nodded again looking into his eyes, which were much softer than the tone of his voice. He was clearly turned on (the hard-on in his pants was a clear indicator) and it surprised her that she was, too. He disappeared behind her.

"Now give me the sign for okay," he said.

She did.

"Good, now the sign for stop."

Again, she made the sign with her bound hands.

"Very good," he said, then he helped her forward a few steps and leaned her over the bench.

It wasn't comfortable, but it wasn't painful either. The top of the bench was padded, but it was still cold and somewhat unyielding. Her stance left her behind and the flesh between her legs exposed. She felt something cold and hard press against the tight pucker of her ass. Panicking, she pushed it out only to discover it slid deeper into her. Pushing out again, she couldn't dislodge it. Whimpering, she tried again. It went even deeper.

"Good girl. Now relax. Remember what I said about letting go?"

Amy closed her eyes and took a deep breath through her nose. She felt the rubber penis in her anus slowly start moving in and out. Eric pulled it all the way out, then put it all the way in. He moved it slowly. Finally, he pushed it all the way in again and left it.

"I know you're uncomfortable," he told her. "But I think it's a good starting point for us to work through your obvious discomfort with certain aspects your sexuality. Don't you?" He gently rubbed the small of her back, and then dragged the flogger lightly over her arms, back, and buttocks. More than anything Amy wanted him inside her.

That thought was only amplified when she felt the flogger smack her across the ass. Then again, and again. Eric wasn't hitting her gently either. It stung and it hurt and she loved it. She felt herself shoving her ass up to meet the flogger each time it struck her.

He finally stopped and ran his hand over her ass. "Mmm. Nice color. I'm not happy with it though. I think maybe you need a good caning."

She moaned and collapsed into her restraints, completely helpless and so turned on. When he finally brought the cane across her ass with tight, quick smacks she screamed in surprise at the pain. The cane hurt like hell and yet she shoved her ass toward it, wanting it. Even with the tears streaking down her face she felt her pussy lubricate again, the wetness dripping from her hole. He worked the cane over her ass cheeks and down the backs of her thighs and finally stopped after the second pass. She breathed a sigh of contented relief. All the anxiety and emotional stress that had been walled up inside her was released and she felt great.

"You're not going to use your safe signal, are you?" His hand rubbed her inner thighs and over her sore ass. "Look at those beautiful welts."

Feeling herself being lifted she relaxed. He pulled the dildo from her ass, undid the ball gag and gently pulled her against him. She wanted him so bad.

"I think that's enough for tonight. Just let me clean up a little and then we'll clean you up. Keep the wrist cuffs on." His eyes slid over her.

She watched as he took all the toys to the sink, sprayed them with something then ran hot water over them. Then he motioned for her to come over.

"Back in the shower."

Stepping into the shower obediently she relaxed and let him deal with the soap and water and washing. She merely closed her eyes and enjoyed it. Admittedly the water against her ass stung at first, but then it felt better. He was very careful to be gentle. Finally, the water turned off and she was wrapped in a towel. Her feet came out from underneath her and she realized he'd picked her up and started toward the stairs. Once out of the basement he put her on her feet.

"Upstairs gorgeous. To bed with you." He paused, turning lights on as they headed up the stairs to the upper level.

She had grabbed her clothes on the way upstairs and lingered in front of him, waiting for him to follow. It wasn't that she wanted to be underfoot, but she didn't know which room he wanted her in. Finally she bit her lip and gave him her best come hither look. "Which room do you want me in, Master?"

He caught up with her in the upstairs hallway and directed her to the master bedroom. "Mine."

Smiling at him, she took his hand and pulled him into the room.

Laughing, he playfully picked her up and tossed her on the bed causing the bath towel to fall off. "Get under the blanket and get some sleep, no funny business," he said with a grin, then went into the bathroom and closed the door.

She tossed her clothes on a chair next to the bed, threw her towel over the chair, and climbed beneath the blankets, inhaling the scent of the sheets. They smelled like him. She closed her eyes and relaxed against the pillows. With a yawn, the world went a little hazy and she drifted off to sleep.

Chapter Seven

"Amy, time to wake up," he whispered in her ear.

She felt a gentle kiss on her cheek. Her eyes fluttered open and she remembered where she was. Looking around she saw Eric, his rock hard chest, chiseled like a Greek god, bare and right next to her. "What time is it?"

"Seven-thirty. There's still some coffee in the pot from last night."

They'd gotten so distracted by each other that she barely recollected the coffee from the night before. "That works. Can I use the bathroom first?"

"I insist." He stayed in bed and watched her get up and walk into the bathroom. "How are those welts feeling?"

Her hand instinctively went back to her ass. She pressed. "Ah! As long as I don't sit or touch them, I'm sure I'll be fine."

"Ha! There are extra toothbrushes under the sink if you want. I'm going to go grab some coffee; I'll bring you a cup."

"Thank you!" She looked at herself in the mirror, and then looked around the massive bathroom. Her new boyfriend had one hell of a house. *If he even wants you anymore now that he's had his way with you in his dungeon, you whore*, her mind told her. She shoved the voice to the back of her head and turned around to inspect the welts. They were deep and red. "Damn," she whispered.

After brushing her teeth and cleaning herself up, she went back into the bedroom to find her bag sitting next to the chair as well. Eric must have brought it up from the kitchen. She had a fresh shirt and a fresh pair of panties in her bag. It was something she always did, carried extra clothes. You just never knew when you were going to need a change of clothing and she was glad she had them. By the time she was dressed, Eric was back with a steaming mug of coffee for her. It had cream and sugar in it, just how she liked it. It was surprising all the things he'd picked up about her in the three weeks they'd known each other. He kissed her and disappeared into the bathroom. The shower turned on.

She brushed her hair, pulling it into a ponytail on the back of her head. Then, using her compact she did her makeup. The area where Emily had hit her the night before was completely unaffected though it was slightly tender to the touch. She finished putting her makeup on and grabbed her bag. The shower turned off.

"Eric, I'm going downstairs."

"Okay, there's more coffee but you'll have to nuke it. Newspaper's on the kitchen table."

She chuckled to herself and carefully wandered back downstairs. The house looked different in the daylight. Brighter, more airy. Bigger. Finding her way to the kitchen didn't prove too difficult. On the way she discovered the laundry room. The light also gave her a better view of the backyard which was large and set up for entertaining. She must have been standing there for a while because Eric came in behind her.

"Do you entertain a lot?" she asked, motioning to the patio with furniture and a large outdoor barbeque pit.

"In the summer, yeah. We have a lot of private parties here and Brad and some of the guys come over a lot. Poker night is always here." He poured himself another cup of coffee.

"Cool." She smiled at him, wondering if she was just his first one night stand since Emily. But technically they hadn't had sex, she reminded herself. Maybe he decided he didn't want to, her insecurity screamed.

"Uh oh, what's the pensive look for?" Eric had a raised eyebrow and he actually looked concerned.

"Just thinking."

The doorbell rang. He gave her a look that said the conversation wasn't over and disappeared to answer it. There was a commotion and laughter in the other room and Eric came back to the kitchen with Brad and Kali in tow. Today Kali was wearing jeans and a t-shirt.

"We brought breakfast. Thought you two might need food since Eric's house is often lacking food unless he's having a party," Kali announced with a smile.

Amy could have died. She thought she'd be able to pull it off. No walk of shame wearing the same exact outfit from the night before. No one would have known that she'd stayed the night at Eric's, and Brad and Kali most certainly knew what they'd been doing.

"Amy, sit, eat," Brad said.

Eric nodded.

As if in response, her ass throbbed. The wooden chairs would not be kind to her welt laden rear. With a cringe she sat. The pain was immediate and then it began to throb some more.

Her reaction didn't go unnoticed by Brad and Kali.

Kali literally leaned over and pulled at the waistband of Amy's jeans. "Stand up."

Amy found herself shuffled to her feet and before she knew what was happening Kali had Amy's jeans undone and pulled halfway down.

"Eric, good God! A little rough for a first play date, don't you think? Look!" Kali turned Amy, showing Brad her ass, covered with the welts from the cane.

Brad just smiled and gave Eric a slight nod.

He just smiled. "Relax, Kali, she's fine."

Amy pulled her pants back up, acutely aware that her face was deep crimson. "I'm fine," she whispered. She felt outnumbered again. She didn't know any other subs. She only knew Doms and now she was stuck between them having breakfast.

This thought, of course, brought up a different question. What the hell were Brad and Kali doing together? When the question hit her, she literally cocked her head and gave Eric a look. She glanced at Brad, then at Kali, and then back to Eric with a shrug.

He started laughing.

Brad and Kali both looked up from their breakfast sandwiches.

Amy's hand went over her mouth to cover the huge grin there. There was no way she was laughing in a room full of Doms.

Brad lifted an eyebrow. "What the hell is with you two?"

Eric shook his head. "Nothing. Private joke between Amy and me."

Amy sat quietly, eating, trying to become as small as possible.

"Kali is going to help us with the inventory tonight," Brad said.

"Oh good. I have to run Amy home after closing first, she has some coursework to get done," he said, glancing at her.

Amy kept her head down, not sure if she should say anything. Instead she finished her breakfast and hid for a few minutes in the downstairs bathroom. The only chance she'd really be able to talk to Eric would be in the car before work, and maybe at the store. Regardless, they had to talk. She was starting to feel a bit uncertain about things. After all, she'd only known Eric for a couple of weeks and here they were, having some sort of whirlwind romance. She laughed. Was that what it was? Romance? Or just kinky sex?

With a groan, she finally emerged from the bathroom to find Eric, Brad and Kali throwing the last of the breakfast trash away and heading toward the door. It was eight fifteen and the store opened at nine.

Once in Eric's car she tried to think of a way to start the conversation, but it wasn't coming to her.

Eric broke the silence first. "Sorry about the Brad and Kali takeover this morning. They sometimes show up for breakfast."

"Are they...?"

Eric laughed. "I sometimes wonder, but that would mean one of them is a switch and to be honest I don't want to know. I just know that sometimes they'll both stop by before work for breakfast. It's sporadic."

Amy shrugged. "They'd make a cute couple, aesthetic-wise."

He smiled. "Yeah? And what about us?"

It was the perfect opportunity. "Oh, I think we're a good match aesthetically speaking."

"And beyond the aesthetics?" he asked; only briefly taking his eyes off the road.

"You mean, are we a couple?" A lump formed in her throat. It was the moment of truth. She was going to find out if she was just a one-night-stand.

"Well yeah. Are we a good match?"

"Well, we're obviously physically attracted to one another. We get along well. We enjoy each other's company," she started. "I think we could be a good match…"

"But?"

Sighing, she decided honesty was the best route. "But we haven't even known each other for very long and I've already been in your bed. What does that say about me?"

He snorted. "If it says something about you it says something about me, too. Are you having a Catholic guilt moment?"

Her brows furrowed. "What's a Catholic guilt moment?"

"That moment when, after you've had what society deems inappropriate sexual contact with someone you've only recently met, you feel a tremendous amount of guilt and regret and begin questioning your morality and what kind of person you are."

"Yeah, I suppose. But I'm not Catholic," she told him.

Laughing, he looked over at her, "So you're regretting last night?"

"No," she started. "It's not that, it's just that I've just always believed in waiting at least a few months before jumping into bed with a guy."

"And you've believed this because?" He frowned when another car cut in front of him, causing him to tap the brakes. "Because our Judeo Christian society preaches no sex until marriage and women who aren't virgins are evil? Or because narrow-minded people would think you were a slut because you went out with a guy only a few weeks after you met him, then had a sexual encounter and slept in the same bed with him?"

"Exactly," she agreed.

"One of the hardest lessons to learn in life is that you can't spend your entire life worrying about what everyone else is going to think or you'll end up not doing anything out of fear of someone else disapproving of your choices. So I have a few questions for you." He paused.

Amy held her breath.

"Do you enjoy hanging out with me outside of work?"

"Yes," she said, and it was true. She really did like Eric and they got along famously. He was funny, interesting and intelligent. Not to mention built and extremely attractive.

"Did you enjoy our sexual encounter last night?"

Her heart almost stopped. "Yes."

"I noticed with the cane you really let go of all those pent up emotions. I think it might be a good alternative to hurting yourself," he said quietly.

Another moment of panic ran through her. He was bringing up *that* uncomfortable subject again. She thought about it. He was right, of course. She had released emotionally. The pain was precisely what she needed so she could cry. She'd actually enjoyed the pain; even got turned on by it. "You have a point."

"Some subs can't properly release emotions without a little help. I'm more than willing to take care of that need whenever you need it," he told her. His eyes held a great deal of concern and warmth.

She nodded. "Okay."

"So you really enjoyed last night then?"

She couldn't deny it. "Yes."

"Good because I enjoy your company and I enjoyed last night. I'd like to keep seeing you and we'll see where it goes. Besides, a lot of people sleep with the person they're dating four or five dates in. As I see it, we spent almost a full three weeks, eight hours every day together, which is longer than a four hour date. So technically we know more about one another than those couples. Right?"

Now it was her turn to laugh. He certainly had a point. For some reason, that point, regardless how lame or contrived a justification, made her feel a great deal better about herself.

"So can I keep seeing you outside of work, Amy Myers?"

A slow smile spread across her lips. "Yes Master Eric."

He let out a sigh of relief. "Good. I was worried you were going to tell me you never wanted to see me again."

She rolled her eyes. "No, I was just going to suggest we slow down a little."

Pulling into the parking lot behind the store, he put the car in park and turned it off, then turned to her. "I thought we were going slowly. We haven't technically had intercourse."

She felt her face turn at least three shades of red. "True, but we were very close. We might as well have."

"I was hoping to build some anticipation to that. I had to take two cold showers last night."

She gave him a broad smile and shook her head. "Well if you put me off too long I can't be held responsible for what I might do." She bit her lip, her gaze subconsciously settling on his crotch.

"Oh really?" He chuckled. "Impetuous little sub. I'm putting that on my list of reasons to give your ass another caning."

The warm tingling of arousal flooded her. As if a reminder, her still sore and welted behind throbbed a little.

"Could we wait until my butt has had time to recover from the last one?"

They started out of the car. "As long as you behave and do as you're told."

While his tone had taken on a serious note, she saw a playful glint in his eye. Wordlessly, she followed him into the store. Brad was already there, but Kali had disappeared. Evidently Brad had dropped her off somewhere along the way.

The day started slow, but as it wore on, business picked up and the time flew by. Amy and Eric didn't have much time to talk and Brad was his usual disciplined self. Before she knew it, it was already six and the store was closed.

"Are you sure you don't want me to stick around for inventory?" she asked.

Eric yawned and shook his head. "Nope. I seem to recall the matter of homework for your classes."

It was true. She had an essay to write and some reading to do. She nodded, also yawning.

"So you guys didn't get much sleep last night?" Brad asked.

"Fuck you, man," Eric said, herding Amy out the back toward the car.

"Don't take forever to get her home," Brad called after them.

Amy felt her face flush. Guys were always so harsh with each other. It was something she didn't think she'd ever get used to.

As they pulled out of the parking lot she saw the familiar car and the familiar face behind the wheel as the car pulled out behind them, but she shrugged it off as her own paranoia. There was no way that after three weeks Paul was still following her. On the way home they talked about their childhoods; Amy sharing her adventures as an only child and Eric stories about tormenting his sister, and his sister getting even. When he dropped her off he waited until she got into the house before driving away.

Amy carefully navigated her parents questions and want for conversation. Finally she found herself in her basement bedroom reading about business ethics and taking notes. By midnight she'd finished the paper and the reading and fell asleep.

It was either the thick smell of smoke or the screaming from outside that woke her. The room was hazy and smoky and there weren't any lights. Panic swelled within her. She tried to turn on the lamp but nothing happened. Reaching around she found her jeans and a t-shirt and pulled them on, staying as low to the ground as possible. Quickly she held her breath and stood, opening the window. She used the handle of a broom to help push out the screens. Absentmindedly she grabbed her backpack and threw it into the window well, then hoisted her thin frame from the room. Then she threw her backpack onto the front lawn. Coughing, she tried to hoist herself out of the window well.

"We've got the young woman! Over here!" A man's voice shouted.

Before she knew what was happening, Amy was pulled from the window well and then she was sitting in the back of an ambulance wearing an oxygen mask. Her parents were there. In front of them the house stood ablaze, crumbling. It was like a bad surreal dream.

At least I saved my homework, she thought. She snorted at the thought. It was absurd. The one thing she saw fit to save was that damn fifty pound backpack filled with her laptop and college textbooks. Finally, her thoughts turned sober when she realized that she and her parents had lost everything they had.

Her father had managed to save his cell phone and his lockbox, her mother a photo album. He'd just finished a phone call to the insurance company and had gotten ahold of his sister when a police officer approached them. "You folks have some place to go?"

"My husband's sister has an apartment in Leichster," her mother said through a veil of tears.

"I'll need that phone number," the officer said, getting the information.

Amy fought the urge to groan. She didn't want to go to her aunt's house. It was a one bedroom apartment which left her father sleeping in the recliner and she and her mom sharing the pull out couch. So when her father was finished with the phone, Amy took the opportunity to make a phone call of her own.

Eric answered promptly in a concerned tone.

"Eric?"

"Amy? What's wrong?"

"How did you know..." she started.

"It's three o'clock in the morning. No one calls at three in the morning unless something's wrong. Where are you? Are you okay?"

"I'm fine," she assured him. Just hearing his voice calmed her and made her feel safe. "It's just my parents' house, not so much. Umm, there was a fire."

He was completely awake now. She could tell because all traces of sleepiness were gone from his voice. "Where are you?"

"On the side of the ambulance with my parents waiting for my aunt to pick us up," she told him.

"I can be there in ten minutes. You can stay with me," he said.

"I don't want you to feel like you have to…"

"I don't *have* to do anything. I *want* to. I'll be there in ten minutes," he said again. Then the phone went dead.

"Amy, I need the phone back. I need to call the auto insurance," her father said.

She handed the phone back to him. "I'm going to go stay with a friend. I don't want to overcrowd Aunt Laura."

Much to her own surprise her parents didn't protest. They also didn't protest when Eric showed up and stood next to Amy, listening as the officer and a fireman discussed how the fire may have started.

"It looks like it may have started on the west side of the house. I'll need to come out tomorrow in the daylight and see if it was faulty wiring or arson," the fireman was saying.

"Arson?" Amy's father asked.

"I can't be sure, but it looks like the fire may have started on the outside wall. There's no electricity on the outside wall," he explained.

Eric put his arm around Amy's waist, pulling her close to him. His touch alone warmed her.

"Did any of you hear anything or notice anyone acting suspiciously?" the officer asked.

Amy and her parents shook their heads.

The officer turned to her then. "What about you, miss? Any angry boyfriends?"

Amy frowned. "Boyfriends? No. Well, my ex, but he hasn't bothered contacting me since I broke up with him about three weeks ago."

"You broke up with Paul?" her mother asked.

"It was over months ago, mom," Amy said, fighting the urge to roll her eyes like an insolent teenager. Their house had just burned down and her mother actually cared that she broke it off with Paul? She let out an exasperated sigh.

"Well, we'll know more after tomorrow. In the meantime if any of you think of anything, contact me." The officer gave her parents a card with his number on it.

Eric pulled his own card out of his wallet and handed it to Amy's father. "That's my number if you guys need to get ahold of Amy."

"I'll be at school and work," she said, dazed. The dazed feeling was starting to overtake her.

"No," Eric said flatly. "You're sleeping in and you can call your professors and let them know what happened. Then maybe you need some family time. You can drive my pickup if you want."

"My license and my purse are burnt to a crisp."

"Then I'll stay home and drive you around and maybe we'll stop at the DMV and get you a replacement. Okay?"

Amy's parents said nothing, just passively watched the exchange.

"Okay," she finally conceded. She was too tired to worry about any of it and thankful that Eric had taken control of the situation.

After a few polite words with her parents and after shaking her father's hand, Eric rejoined her and led her to the car, helping her in. Throwing her backpack into the back seat he got in and pulled away from the home she'd grown up in. Amy felt the familiar numb sensation slowly make its way through her, dragging her into the darkness. She hadn't felt this way since high school. Finally they were pulling into his driveway.

There were two other cars there.

Eric physically had to open the passenger door and lift her out. Her legs didn't want to work. There were voices and people talking but she couldn't focus on any of them. It was all a blur. She didn't have any clothes. No makeup. Not even a toothbrush or a comb. She was homeless. Her parents were homeless. They'd lost even more than her. After all, she was just a college student who didn't have a lot to begin with other than a wardrobe, some odds and ends furniture, a few nick knacks and memorabilia from her childhood. For her parents, however, their home was something they'd spent a lifetime building. At least all their lives had been spared. They could replace things, but they couldn't replace each other.

"Amy, are you okay?" a female voice said.

"I'm fine," she heard herself say in a hollow, dead voice."

"That's not fine," the familiar man's voice said.

"No, she'll be fine," Eric insisted. "Maybe after some sleep."

"You're the one who told me about the scars and how she reacted to the cane. You can't tell me this isn't shutting down," the man's voice said. "She's got a history of it, Eric. If you don't pull her out she could try to hurt herself."

"Maybe I should hide all the knives," the woman said.

"Let's see if she comes out of it on her own," Eric said with some uncertainty.

"I know this is the first time you've had a sub with this particular need. You have to learn to recognize the signs. I've seen this before. She's completely shut down, Eric," said a familiar male voice.

"She just needs some sleep," Eric said again, not sounding entirely convinced.

"Come on, we'll take you upstairs and get you tucked in," the female said.

"I'm fine," Amy repeated. Obediently, her legs moved, following the blurry figure. Her feet felt like rubber. Her emotions were numb. She just couldn't feel anything. They went up the stairs. There were footfalls behind her, but she didn't turn around. She didn't care.

Then she was in the bedroom. It was Eric's room, she remembered.

"Amy," came Eric's voice from her left.

Amy sucked in a ragged breath and continued to stare forward. She remembered the smoke and the heat and the strange whooshing sound. That horrible sound; it was the fire devouring everything. She'd been so close to dying. She sucked in another rough breath.

She felt pressure on her face, a slight sting on her cheek. "Amy!" the woman's voice came at her.

The smoke. The thick acrid smoke. It filled her lungs and burned. She smelled like it. Her chest tightened. A cool breeze slid over her body as her clothes were removed. Then she was walking again. The tile beneath her feet was cold and hard. She stood in the small space, warm water raining down on her, but she still felt cold.

She felt the hands working the towel over her body, drying her off.

"It's not working you guys," the woman said. "Eric, Brad's right. I've seen this before a couple of times."

With a sigh Eric put his face inches from Amy's. "Amy, sweetheart, focus. Do you see me?"

She nodded. Through the darkness she saw Eric and only Eric. The numbness was starting to scare her. More than anything she wanted to dig into her skin with her nails and rip away the flesh to make the darkness go away.

"Are you going to hurt yourself?" Eric asked. "Is pain the only thing that will bring you out of this?"

Again, she nodded. She needed to cry. If only she could cry. Forcing her emotions, she tried to. She thought of all the saddest things that had ever happened to her. Nothing was working.

"There, you have your answer," the man said. "It has to be done."

Why couldn't she tell who it was? She knew him. The darkness spiraled around her.

"Amy, give me your hands," it was Eric's voice again. His order comforted her.

She offered her hands toward the sound of his voice. She felt the wrist cuffs go on.

"I don't know if I can do this," Eric said.

"You can't let her shut down, Eric. She needs to be brought back, otherwise she could hurt herself. I've seen this before," the male voice told him. "Trust me, this isn't medical shock. I'm a trained paramedic, remember? This is an emotional shut down. A few stings from the whip and she's going to come right out of it, I promise."

"I agree with Brad," the female voice said.

Amy's arms were hoisted over her head and she was restrained there, by the wrist cuffs. She wasn't uncomfortable or anything. She just was.

The first few stings of the whip on her back and ass didn't hurt at all. As a matter of fact the sensation was exquisite. It gave her satisfaction. The sensation then built to a crescendo, like something was going to burst out of her chest. That's when she felt the first sting of searing pain and she cried out.

"You have to keep going," the familiar male voice said.

The whip came across her lower back. With that the room came into sharp focus and for the first time since she crawled out of the window well, she was fully present in reality. With a sickening crack the whip hit her square on the buttocks. She cried out as the pain radiated through the already tender flesh. With the pain, the reality of the night came rushing into her now lucid mind. She collapsed against the restraints, sobbing. Sobbing because she could have lost her parents. She could have died. They'd lost everything and there was a possibility that someone had set the house on fire *on purpose*. The tears flowed freely now and she was aware of Kali, who released her wrists, and Eric whose arms she fell into. She also became aware of Brad who was carefully coiling the whip back up.

"That's better, let it out, Amy."

Kali grabbed a blanket from the chair and gave it to Eric, who wrapped Amy into it, clutching her to his chest.

She cried for at least an hour before finally falling asleep in Eric's arms.

She woke to find herself in Eric's bed, warm and safe and nestled against his chest. His soft breath and embrace comforted her. She stretched out alongside his body, pushing herself as close to him as she could. Her gaze traveled to the bedside table to the blue numbers on the alarm clock. It was eleven thirty! Jumping up she looked around. She'd already missed classes and Eric had missed work. That's when what had happened the night before flooded back to her.

Eric sat up behind her. "Amy, lay back down. Rest. You had a long night." His hand slid over her shoulders and back and he gently pulled her back into the bed. He kissed the back of her head and she relaxed against him.

"I wonder if I should call my mom and see how my parents are doing," she whispered.

"I talked to your mom this morning," he said. "I didn't want to wake you and she didn't want me to wake you but she said not to worry about anything. All she and your dad are doing today is meeting with insurance people and talking to the fire inspector. You have been ordered to get some rest and then if you want, you should go to your Aunt Laura's and have dinner."

She let out an exasperated sigh. "I don't want to. I don't have any damn thing to wear..."

"Kali guessed your size and got with some of her girlfriends early this morning and pulled you together some clothes. They're hanging in the closet," he said into the back of her neck.

"Don't you have to go to work?"

"Brad is taking today and we've got a friend coming in to help out."

"You have an answer for everything."

"Yep." He let out a contented sigh. "Now sleep a little longer, would you? I'm enjoying it."

She closed her eyes and tried, but sleep never came back. Instead, she listened to Eric's heartbeat and relaxed against the gentle rise and fall of his chest as he slept. Finally, when she couldn't stay in bed anymore she got up and went directly to the shower. Once she was finished she slipped into the huge walk-in closet which had been half empty when she'd last seen it. Now, the entire right side had a good selection of women's clothing. A smile crossed her lips as she looked at the clothes. They were a combination of casual and conservative. With Kali at the helm of that decision making she half expected to see latex and leather. Though there were a few tasteful mini-skirts. Evidently Eric had shared his love of short skirts with Kali, too? She wondered. Not today, no, today she decided to wear jeans and a soft pink button down blouse. Several new pairs of panties and bras in her size also sat there, along with shoes. They'd thought of everything. The thoughtfulness touched her deeply. None of her friends had ever been this kind and thoughtful before. *Then maybe you need to update your friends*, her mind responded.

Then she thought back to the night before. She had needed to cry and the sting of the whip was the only thing able to bring it out of her. She'd almost emotionally shut down and gone to a dark place, and yet the three of them had kept her from falling. The whole experience gave her a new view of dominance and submission. Did all Doms have the same need to dominate and care for their subs as Eric seemed to care for her? Certainly that was the case since Brad and Kali both seemed just as concerned for her and as thoughtful about her welfare as Eric did. More importantly, did all subs feel the same need she did to submit to a master? Did they all feel that need to please and care for a Dom like she did Eric? While Amy gladly acknowledged that something inside her had changed and that she now understood her own submission better, there was something special about Eric. She was happy their relationship had happened and she wanted it. All of it. But it still scared her a little bit.

Despite the fact that she had no home, no money, no driver's license, and not a single possession (minus her backpack, textbooks and laptop and the student loan that came with college), she still had a lot to be thankful for. She still had her parents, her friends, a wonderful boyfriend and a good job. At that moment she felt safe, secure, happy, fortunate, grateful and well rested. Slipping quietly downstairs she made a pot of coffee and enjoyed the view of the backyard from the kitchen table. When Eric came up behind her she didn't even flinch in surprise.

He kissed her cheek. "How are we this morning my sweet Amy?"

She smiled up at him. "Fine. Happy to be alive. Thank you for not letting me fall into that dark place."

He hugged her tightly and kissed the top of her head. "I didn't want to use the whip on you at all. If it hadn't been for Brad and Kali…"

"It's okay. I needed it," she admitted; and she did. The bite of the whip was the only alternative to hurting herself. She knew it and she was pretty sure Eric did, too.

"Oh, Kali said if we drop by the DMV off fifth they can make you a duplicate license there. It shouldn't take us more than forty-five minutes if the line is long," he said, going over to the coffee pot and pouring himself a cup. "Soon as I've had some coffee I'll run upstairs, get ready, and we'll go. Twenty minutes, tops."

"Okay."

"Are you feeling numb or distant?" he asked. His eyes were filled with a great deal of concern.

"No. I'm comfortable," she decided. "I don't want to do anything, but I suppose I should call my aunt's house and see what's up."

Eric nodded. "You do that and I'm off to get ready."

After he disappeared upstairs she picked up the phone and called her aunt only to learn they were having dinner at six and she should bring Eric. Getting a replacement drivers license didn't take as long as she anticipated and as scheduled, she and Eric showed up at her aunt Laura's just before six to find her parents and Paul waiting for her.

Amy's jaw tightened. The sight of Paul pissed her off and she wondered what the hell he was doing there. Eric noticed her immediate change in mood and put on a big smile.

Once they were all seated around the table, looking at each other over plates of her aunt Laura's famous lasagna, Amy couldn't hold back anymore. "So is there a reason you invited both Paul and Eric to a family dinner after the house burned down?"

Her father looked nervous. "Amy, we need to talk to you. We found out something today..."

Amy's eyes narrowed. She glanced at Paul who was giving Eric threatening looks. Eric remained calm with a reserved expression plastered on his face. "Well spit it out," she said, her voice cold.

"We found out the fire was no accident. It was set *on purpose*. As it turns out Paul here was driving by while we were at the house today and he stopped. He was concerned for your well-being and told us you were hanging out with some bad people. No offense intended toward Eric, but I need to know exactly who he is, how come your mother and I have never heard about him before, and what kind of shady things he's into." Her father looked directly at Eric when he said that.

She paused for a moment like a deer caught in the headlights. First, the fact that the fire wasn't an accident was definitely concerning. Second, Paul... she couldn't even finish the thought because it filled her with such rage. Taking a deep breath she finally said, "Paul's just angry because I dumped him so he's created bullshit stories about Eric. Eric is my boss and a friend. The nature of our relationship beyond that really isn't anyone's business unless we choose to make it their business."

Paul stood up and started toward her. "You *are* sleeping with him! I knew it! You were cheating on me the whole time with this freaky fucker?"

Eric stood, calmly locking his hand around Paul's wrist and directing him back toward his chair. In that deep calming Dom voice he said, "Sit down. Let's not start anything or let tempers get out of control."

Pulling his wrist away, Paul glared at Eric. "You got her hooked up with the S and M crowd."

As if unbidden, Eric's left eyebrow lifted, begging Paul to continue.

"I followed you two to *Black Lily*. Everyone knows what goes on *there*. Did you turn her into one of your whores? Are you beating her?" Paul challenged.

Eric's expression turned hard. "I would never hurt Amy and I resent the implication that I'm abusive toward her in any way."

Paul leaned around Eric and looked Amy square in the eyes. "Has he hurt you?"

Amy's mouth was hanging open. She knew it and made no move to close it. She just didn't have the words. Had she known Paul was following her... she felt her face turning red with anger. That's when she noticed her parents looking at her. "No! Eric has never hurt me. What the hell?"

"Have you been to that club?" Her father asked in a subdued tone.

"Well, yeah, we stopped by there for a drink with some of our friends Saturday night. We didn't go into the back or participate. Damn, Paul, if you're going to talk crap about me to my parents at least get your story straight. I have two more friends who will tell you it was only drinks." She gave Eric an apologetic look.

"He owns the damn club!" Paul challenged.

Amy swallowed the lump in her throat. Paul had been a busy little beaver.

Eric shook his head. "Correction - I am an investor in that club, but I also co-own a bookstore, a furniture store, and I've invested in a movie production company and a micro-brewery. I don't keep my eggs in one basket. I find it makes more financial sense to spread out into different areas," he said in a very professional, business-like tone. "And yes, Amy and I are dating. But I didn't ask her out until you were out of the picture. Truth is, man, she was thinking about dumping you weeks before she actually did it."

She nodded. "True."

"Then if everything you say is true, Amy won't have any problem showing us her back. Or at least taking her mother and aunt in the other room to show she doesn't have bruises or marks on her from this asshole beating her," Paul said triumphantly.

A swell of panic rose in the pit of Amy's stomach. She hoped the panic she felt wasn't written across her face. Even Eric shifted uncomfortably in his chair. There was no hiding the marks from the whip the night before or the caning from the night before that. "Well that's a dumb idea," she finally said.

"I don't think it's unreasonable and it would give your mother and I some piece of mind," her father said.

"No, it's a dumb idea because I do have bruises and scrapes on my body after climbing out of a small basement window and trying to climb out of a window well. The rose bush caught my back," She stood up and showed them the real bruises from her climb to safety. They were on her forearms, and gave them a peak at her back under her shirt. It sounded plausible to her at least. After all, when she'd seen her own back in the mirror that morning she mused that's what the whip marks looked like. Like she'd fallen into a rose bush. She was hoping her parents wouldn't be any the wiser.

"In that case all the more reason for your mother and aunt to take a look, go." Her father dismissed her with a wave of his hand and turned to Eric.

Amy got up and started to follow her mother and aunt down the hallway but she stopped short. "Wait a minute. Why am I doing this? I'm an adult. I'm over twenty-one. You can't force me into a strip search." She turned around and grabbed her jacket and bag, generously supplied by the industrious Kali. "Come on Eric, we're leaving."

"Amy, if you leave this house..." her father started.

Eric got up and followed her toward the door.

She stopped, "If I leave what?"

"If you leave before we know what's going on I'm going to have to tell the police everything Paul knows so they can catch the arsonist who burned down the house."

She whirled around, really angry now. "So you're saying that just because my boyfriend invests in a club, just because I went there for drinks and just because I won't submit to a strip search that somehow that's why the house was burned down?"

"If you're hanging out with people who are of a criminal element, yes," her father concluded.

Paul nodded vigorously in agreement.

"Criminal element?" Amy rolled her eyes, ignoring Eric's imploring look. He clearly didn't want her to make things worse, but the truth was being honest and knowing it would be shocking and scary and upset her family, and even more so Paul, made her feel powerful no matter what miserable consequences came of it. "Fine. I *am* into bdsm, but only with Eric. I have a couple other friends into the scene, but neither of them would have burned the house down. The only reason Paul saw fit to stalk me was because I dumped his lame ass. If it weren't for that neither of you would have had any clue what my private sex life entailed. Thanks for that, Paul. I hope you're satisfied that I'm absolutely embarrassed and mortified that my parents know more about my sex life than they should. So in the same spirit I'll say in front of everyone present that you're lame in bed and couldn't find the clitoris if you were given a map. The reason I dumped you is because you treated me like a good for nothing whore. Eric has never treated me like that - ever!"

Taking a startled Eric by the hand, they left the apartment and soon found themselves sitting in the car in silence.

"Well that was... shocking?" Eric finally concluded.

"Does your family know you're into bdsm?" she asked.

He shook his head. "Hell no. I can't imagine what I'd say or do if they ever found out."

She shrugged. "I have nothing and therefore have nothing to lose."

Turning to her he took her hand into his. "That's not true. You've got me, and Brad, and whether you like it or not, I think Kali has taken a liking to you, too."

"Well, I'm going to have to find a new place to live, ugh. I don't want to think about it." She looked out the window. She watched her aunt's apartment complex disappear in the side view mirror as he pulled out of the parking lot and turned onto the main road.

There was a pregnant pause. "You can stay with me for as long as you want."

"Yeah, but that's an imposition..." she started.

"Amy, were you serious about wanting to have a relationship with me?"

"Well, yeah, but it's moving too fast," she told him.

He was silent for a few minutes. "I see your point, I do. But there are people who get married after knowing each other a month or two. I'm not suggesting anything that rash. Just living together. You can even have one of the spare bedrooms if sharing a bedroom is too strange for you. You can call me your roommate with benefits if that's what you want."

The lump in her throat was back again. This time accompanied by heartburn from the bite of lasagna she'd managed before all hell broke loose. "I have to think about it."

He nodded. "Okay. Fair enough. Now let's go get some dinner. After that revelation I'm starving and I don't want to deal with policemen on my doorstep without something in my stomach."

Chapter Eight

The police never showed up at Eric's, instead, they showed up at the bookstore the following day. Amy had stopped by the college and talked to all of her professors that morning. Now, she sat doing the makeup homework. There was no way she was leaving her courses unfinished. The student loan people didn't care if she finished a semester or not. She still had to pay them back. The two plain-clothes detectives, a woman and a man, looked like customers at first. Both were dressed in jeans, boots, and solid colored shirts. Amy looked up from her textbook, set it aside and forced a smile. "Welcome to *By The Book*. Can I help you find something?"

"Actually we're looking for Amy Myers and Eric Parsons," the man said. As if they shared some unspoken cue, both detectives flashed their badges. "I'm Detective Tafts and this is Detective Graves."

She fought the urge to give a heavy sigh. "Well, I'm Amy Myers and Eric Parsons is coming up on your left."

"What can we help you with today, detectives?" Eric said with a grin.

"Arson." Detective Tafts looked at Amy and then at Eric. "Can I speak to you privately Mr. Parsons?"

Eric shrugged. "Sure, come on over here."

Detective Graves took a step toward the counter and gave Amy a reassuring smile. "So how long have you been working here?"

"A little over three weeks now," she said, pretending to look at a receipt.

"So you've known Mr. Parsons for..."

"A while," Amy finished.

"So does Mr. Parsons hit you?" The detective put a hand on Amy's shoulder.

"Seriously? Did my parents tell you that?" She rolled her eyes. "My stupid ex-boyfriend, who's stalking me by the way, saw fit to share my personal sexual fetishes with my family. My family, thinking I must be under the influence of someone or something else, can't understand my personal tastes, and so they assume that I'm being abused because it's the only way they can wrap their heads around it. For the record Detective, I'm over twenty-one, I was only living with my parents because I was going to school, and what Eric and I do in the bedroom is consensual. So don't think you're going to get into my head and convince me how abused or mental I am, because I'm neither. I like it rough. A lot of women do and last I heard that wasn't a crime."

The detective nodded and her tone turned from soft to firm. "Do you know of anyone who would want to hurt you?"

"You mean aside from my ex-boyfriend who is incredibly upset that I dumped him for Eric? No. Well," she paused and then remembered the incident with Emily. "Well, no. Eric has a psycho ex-girlfriend, too. She hit me the other night at the club, in the bathroom. But I'm pretty sure she's not the type to burn down houses. I'd almost bet on my ex-boyfriend."

"And why is that? Did he ever hit you?"

"No, but I thought he was going to when I dumped him. Just a look he sometimes gave me when we were together and I wouldn't bend to his will. Like when I wouldn't have sex with him. He was a jerk," she paused thoughtfully. "Though I don't know, maybe he wouldn't do anything like that either. I mean, it could have been just some random freak thing that some arsonist chose our house for burning, couldn't it?"

The detective shrugged. "Anything is possible. Now back to Mr. Parson's ex. What happened there? She followed you into the bathroom? Were there witnesses?"

Amy nodded. "Oh yeah. My friend Kali was there and had Emily removed from the club. She's not allowed back there. She was pretty pissed about it too because she showed up at Eric's house later that night demanding an explanation and telling him how much she loved him. But she left when he told her to."

The detective listened, taking down all the information. Then, Detective Tafts pulled her aside and they compared notes. Eric went back to helping a customer. His jaw was set. Undoubtedly the detective had asked him questions implying he was abusive. Finally, both detectives made their way back over to Amy and Detective Tafts motioned Eric over to them. When they were all assembled the detective eyed them warily. "So we're going to question Paul Marks again. Now what is Emily's last name?"

"Emily?" Eric's face was blank.

"Your ex-girlfriend," the detective clarified.

A sudden shock of realization ran across Eric's face. "Emily Stottle."

After getting as much information as they could about both exes Detective Tafts put his notepad away in his pocket. "We'll start there, but if either of you think of anything, call us."

With that, Eric and Detective Tafts exchanged business cards and the detectives left.

Brad came up from his desk behind the counter. "What the fuck was that?"

She frowned. "It's a long story." Taking some books off the counter she hurried off into the stacks to get some work done. She didn't want to talk about it or think about it.

Eric stayed behind. She heard them talking but she couldn't hear what they were saying since they were both speaking in hushed whispers.

The day couldn't end soon enough. By the time nine o'clock rolled around she was tired and ready to go home. Her new home. That thought alone brought back the stress of the sudden change in her situation. Before she could stop it, that same feeling of numbness seemed to be coming back. She tried to fight it, but she couldn't.

She sat patiently waiting while Brad and Eric locked up. Finally, scared, she whispered, "Eric, I'm not feeling so good."

Brad was closer. He looked into her eyes. "No, you're not. Eric, Amy is shutting down again."

Eric came out from the back room. "Oh babe, not again." Leaning down he helped her up, taking her into the back room.

Brad followed just in case Eric needed his help.

Carefully he removed her jeans and panties.

She barely felt the coolness of the air on her skin. The world started going foggy.

"Over the bench," he said, draping her carefully over one of the benches. He didn't bother restraining her. "Flogger," he said.

Clearly Brad didn't agree, but he gave Eric the flogger anyway.

Eric's hand lightly caressed the area to be flogged.

Amy only felt a light soreness. Then the flogger came across her ass, harder and harder until the sting finally brought her back. Eric gave her a few hard open palm swats with his hand to supplement. That did it. The pain was intense. The tears started flowing and she felt such a great sense of relief she began laughing. Brad brought a blanket over and gave it to Eric who threw it around her shoulders.

"It's okay, babe," he whispered. "Though I really wish you'd use your safe word."

With a sniffle she said, "But it needs to hurt. I need to feel. I need to cry."

"Yeah, well I don't think you're going to tolerate any more whips this week, gorgeous. I'm cutting you off so you can't shut down like this, oaky? We need to find a better way...at least until your body has had some recovery time." He rubbed her back gently, pulling her into his chest.

Amy's head swam. Something sparked inside her and suddenly she was ravenous for him. Her body was on fire and she wanted him, right there, right now. Not caring that Brad was right there in the room with them, her lips found Eric's and she kissed him, pushing her tongue into his mouth. She felt his arousal on her thigh and her hand slipped down to touch it. She ran her fingers its entire length before his hand caught hers and pulled it away.

"I thought *I* was moving too fast?" he challenged.

"Take me now, Master," she whispered breathlessly. Her heart slammed in her chest. She was so turned on what slipped out of her mouth next surprised even her. "I want you, but I want Brad, too. Both of you, at the same time."

Eric's eyes went wide. "Oh. Well, for a threesome we're heading to the home dungeon, if Brad agrees, that is."

Brad actually laughed. It was a surprised laugh, but it was still a laugh. "I need to check with someone first to see if she minds sharing me."

Eric lifted an eyebrow at him, and then turned back to her.

Amy ran her hands through Eric's hair. "Why not here?"

"Don't be greedy or all you'll be getting tonight is a mouthful of cock, if you're lucky." Eric's voice had changed to that rough, sexy Dom voice again.

It made her want to melt into the floor and do whatever he asked of her.

Brad left the room with his cell phone in hand. She could hear him talking to someone.

"I'll be good," she said, quickly pulling her panties and jeans back on so they could leave.

"Are you sure you want a threesome?" He lifted an eyebrow at her.

She nodded. "I just want to know what it's like, Master. I thought since you and Brad are friends and he's seen me naked in a cage…"

Eric grinned.

Once Brad had agreed, the drive home took too long, and making their way to the dungeon took even longer. Or so it seemed.

"Do you still want to do this?" Eric asked her again once they were in the dungeon.

The fire burning in her belly told her she did. She nodded. "Yes, Master."

"Good. You will follow Brad's orders as if they were given by me directly and you will refer to him as Sir. Is that clear."

"Yes, Master."

Brad seemed to hang back, waiting for his cue. After all, she was Eric's sub and this was his dungeon and Brad seemed to respect that.

"Take your clothes off," Eric ordered.

Amy stripped down and stood naked before them, her arms at her sides, her hands balled into fists.

"Present your wrists for the leather cuffs," Eric ordered, handing the cuffs to Brad to put on her.

Amy did as instructed and watched as Brad expertly fastened the wrist cuffs. With the anticipation of her situation dripping down her inner thighs she sighed deeply, enjoying the feeling of being nude and exposed before Brad and Eric. Vulnerable. Now even more so with the wrist cuffs, knowing they could restrain her at any moment and she'd be helpless to stop them.

"Now," Eric said in that calm, practiced way. "Let's put you over one of the benches and take a nice look at that tight asshole of yours. Perhaps we'll start off by taking turns fucking it."

Amy almost fainted dead away right there. His words, though crass and dirty, turned her on even more. The memory of the dildo in her ass made her clench and at the same time, she wanted it. Wanted to be used. Wanted to please them.

Bent over the bench she couldn't see what they were doing. Then Brad moved up to where she could see him. He pulled his thick cock from his pants. "Put it in your mouth," he ordered.

She did as she was told, taking all of him into her mouth to the back of her throat, almost gagging. From behind her she heard Eric opening a condom wrapper. When his penis pressed against the tight ring of her ass, she flinched slightly, tensing up. A muffled whimper escaped her. Brad pulled her hair away from her face, petting her as she took him into her mouth over and over again.

"Relax, babe," she heard Eric say from behind her.

She tried to force herself to relax. Slowly, he made it past the tight ring of muscle and slipped into her. A small cry hovered in the back of her throat as he worked himself in and out of her ass slowly at first, then speeding up. Meanwhile, Brad's cock only seemed to get harder and harder in her mouth. Finally, he pulled it out. "I'll wait to come in your ass," he said.

A flood of warmth ran through her belly and through every inch of her sex. She felt Eric spasm against her with a groan and he leaned into her. He pulled out and she heard him take the condom off while Brad put one on. Brad didn't waste any time and immediately buried his cock in her ass. Laying there helpless she had no choice but to be present, fully, feeling every solid inch slide in and out of her. She moaned, feeling Eric's hand on her head.

He leaned down toward her and kissed her cheek. "Do you like that?"

"Yes, Master," she said with a moan. God, it was so good that she wanted Eric inside her pussy.

"Good, we're going to try something else," he said as if reading her mind. Then he unbound her from the bench. "Let's bring her over here to one of the wedges."

Brad pulled out of her, lifting her up, and gently guided her toward a wedge shaped cushion. Then Eric motioned for Brad to lay back on one of them. He did, his penis still hard and sheathed in a condom. Pulling apart Amy's legs and ass cheeks, they gently guided her back onto Brad's swollen cock. This time it slid in a great deal easier, probably because she had been sufficiently stretched open. She felt him inside her, the anticipation building for Eric to fill her pussy. She wanted him so bad it hurt. Leaning back against Brad she kept her legs spread wide, her sex exposed for Eric's approval. Keeping her hands to her sides, she let Brad shift her weight to where he wanted her.

Eric slipped on another condom, positioned himself between her legs pushed himself into her, slowly, gently. He held her gaze with his eyes. She cried out, wanting to furiously thrust forward, but Brad's hands were on her hips, holding her fast so she could scarcely move. Having both men inside her at once was uncomfortable at first until they were able to find a rhythm. Her clit pulsated in time with the large cocks thrusting in and out of her.

Eric and Brad seemed to have it all worked out. Just when Amy felt she wanted to thrust her hips forward to get some clitoral stimulation, Brad's fingers found her clit. He began massaging her. Then everything went blurry and all Amy felt was the exquisite pleasure of being full, being used and the fingers gently massaging her swollen nub, bringing her higher and higher into ecstasy. The pleasure built and swelled and before she realized what was happening that intense sensation of orgasm overtook her, shooting through her body to the tips of her toes, breasts and fingers. She heard the loud moans and screams of pleasure, not really realizing they were coming from her at first. Brad continued to rub her as both men followed suit, losing control and pounding into her with wild abandon, rocking against her with their own orgasms. When they were all spent they took a moment to regain their bearings.

"Now into the shower with you, then upstairs to the kitchen to make some coffee," Eric told her.

She jumped up, eager to follow her new directive.

Chapter Nine

Eric had already left for work and Amy's class for the day wasn't until ten fifteen. She was looking at the phone, realizing that her parents hadn't even attempted to contact her since the fiasco at her aunt's the night before when the doorbell rang. She started toward the door with a smile, and then paused; reminding herself she needed to see who it was first. She didn't want to run across Emily and end up with a black eye or a busted lip. So before opening the door she looked out the peephole and smiled again when she saw Kali.

As usual, Kali was dressed to the hilt. Her auburn hair was slicked back and shiny. This time she was decked out in black leather. Her blood red lips and nails coupled with the black sunglasses made her look like a model in a magazine ad. Amy paused to take it all in. "I love your boots, Mistress."

"Oh, have you jumped to twenty-four-seven play already?"

She blushed. "No, I guess I'm just kind of getting used to calling you Mistress."

"Can't say I mind, can I come in? You have coffee? I'm dying for a cup."

Amy stepped aside allowing Kali into the house. She closed and locked the door behind her.

"What time is your first class?"

"Hour-and-a-half." Amy told her, wondering if this was a social visit or if Kali was here for a reason.

"Let's go shopping instead," Kali suggested with a smile.

"I don't know," Amy started. She had already skipped classes a few days in the past couple of weeks and didn't want to make it a habit.

"Oh come on. Your house just burned down. I'm sure your professors will give you a little lead way. Besides, you need some girl time. Oh…" she held up a hand as if she'd just had a great idea. "We can go get facials."

"I have to be to work by one."

She rolled her eyes. For thirty-something, Kali still looked like she was in her twenties. "Brad and Eric won't mind. I heard you guys had a little fun last night."

Amy felt the heat rush to her cheeks. Oh God, how did Kali find out? "They told you about that?"

"Not exactly. I talked to my Brad. He called me beforehand to make sure I was cool with it."

Amy's jaw dropped. "You and Brad are hooking up! I knew it!"

Kali shrugged. "Guilty. He's so cute, don't you think? Totally worth being a switch for."

She knew she was gaping at Kali because Kali stopped filling her coffee cup half way.

"You know what a switch is?"

She was sure she kind of knew, but she shook her head just in case. "Not really."

"Well, I am a Domme. I do love having a sub. However, for the right guy I am more than willing to switch sides," she said with a small grin and a wink.

"So how long have you and Brad been…?"

"We hooked up the other night at the club after you and Eric left. Of course it was only a matter of time. We've been eyeing each other and dancing around our mutual attraction for a while. After all, two Doms hooking up rarely happens. I promise though, even though I find Eric absolutely gorgeous, I would never move in on your man. Unless, of course, I had your blessing."

Amy wasn't sure how she felt about that. After all, Kali had given Brad her blessing to enjoy a session with her and Eric. What if she expected Amy to extend that same favor?

"You're cute when you're thinking." She sipped the coffee in her cup. "Hey, so where's Eric's playroom? I've never been invited…"

Amy's eyes instinctively went to the door leading downstairs from the family room.

Kali followed her eyes. She set down the coffee cup. "Oh, just a peek!"

"I don't know. Master, I mean Eric, doesn't want me down there unless he's here," Amy said, wishing she hadn't let Kali in.

"Well what Master Eric doesn't know won't hurt him. Come on, just a peek. You can come with me and keep me out of trouble," Kali suggested.

While every thought in her mind screamed no, the part of her that wanted – no – needed a friend said yes. That's the side that won out because Amy found herself following Kali down into the dungeon.

Kali found the light with ease and hurried down the steps, clearly excited by what she saw. "Very nice! This is the ultimate dungeon. He has everything!" She moved over to the whips and ran her hands over them.

Amy looked around. This was really the first time she'd actually looked at the room as a room. It felt strange being down there without Eric, but it also gave her a new perspective. It wasn't nearly as overwhelming now.

"It looks a lot different when you aren't naked and tied up to something, doesn't it?" Kali shrugged. "Brad's dungeon is well equipped, too, but not like this. He doesn't have an exam table. Awesome for oral, don't you agree?"

She blushed again and shrugged. "Yeah, I suppose."

Kali disappeared around the corner to the part of the dungeon Amy had never seen. "He actually has a filtered water machine down here along with the biggest selection of toys... have you seen this?"

"No." She didn't dare step another foot into the room.

"Amy?" Kali poked her head out from around the corner. "Come on, big chicken. What do you think Eric is going to do if he catches you down here?"

"Umm, I don't know, give me a good spanking?"

She laughed. "Which you'd love, so come here!"

With some reluctance and a wary backward glance at the open door at the top of the stairs, she followed Kali into the other part of the room. There was a loveseat, a water cooler, and a huge dresser full of toys. Kali was going through the drawers.

"Oh wow. Double head dildo! Righteous. Nipple clamps, have you ever tried these?"

Amy shook her head.

"Ugh, you're so Catholic, girl. Live a little!" Kali handed her the nipple clamps. "Try them on – they're to die for."

Standing there holding the chain with a clamp at either end, she held it up and examined it. "What do you do with it?"

Kali started laughing. "Take off your shirt."

"I don't know, you know, we should really get out of here," Amy started.

The older woman rolled her eyes.

"What?" Amy protested. "Why did you look at me like that?"

"You think you're all sexually free just because you let Eric tie you up and whip you. But really, you're still pretty repressed," Kali said matter-of-fact.

"Well I'm not afraid it's just that," she paused, not knowing what to say.

"You're uncomfortable without your top on with another woman in the room?"

"There's that, and," she sighed, not finishing the sentence.

"Just take off your top and your bra. It will be fun." Kali gave her a reassuring smile.

Amy shrugged and began peeling her top off. Once she slid the bra off her ample chest, her nipples immediately hardened.

Kali took the nipple clamps and touched Amy's breast, causing her to jump. "Relax, it's just me. I'm just going to show you how they go on." With that, she squeezed Amy's nipple between her thumb and forefinger until it was nice and hard then attached the small clamp to it.

It hurt at first and Amy realized she was wincing again. She waited while Kali firmly attached the second clamp to Amy's other nipple.

Kali gently tugged on the chain, sending shots of pleasure through Amy's chest and straight down between her thighs.

"There you are. They look hot on you. I bet once Eric gets a set of clamps on you and sees how hot you are with them he won't let you take them off." Kali tugged at the chain again causing Amy to whimper involuntarily.

"But there's something even better you have to try," Kali licked her red lips. She took hold of the chain gently, but with enough pressure that Amy had no choice but to follow her to the exam table. "Lay back."

That's when Amy realized Kali had a pair of wrist cuffs. She didn't struggle as Kali put the cuffs on her then bound her hands above her head. Wordlessly, Kali pulled off Amy's jeans and panties and put her feet in the stirrups.

"Wait here."

Amy felt the weight of the nipple clamps and a rush of panic realizing she'd just allowed Kali to restrain her. Her eyes traveled to the open door at the top of the stairs.

"You worried he's going to come home and find you naked and spread for me?" Kali wore a lustful smile. "Maybe I should call him and tell him to come home because I have a surprise for him." She set a few things down on a small tray set next to the exam table.

Opening her mouth, nothing came out.

With a tube of lube in one hand and a large black butt plug in the other, Kali smiled at her. "Cat got your tongue sweetie? I suppose you could say it's never wise to follow a Domme, switch or not, into a dungeon. What a gorgeous pussy you have and a nice ass that looks like it's been well used." Kali slid a few fingers over Amy's labia, causing her to squirm.

Amy watched in fascination as Kali squirted a glob of lube on the butt plug and smeared it onto it.

"This one vibrates. That's going to feel real good," Kali told her as she pressed the hard tip of the plug into Amy's tight hole. After some pressure and the pain of the wide flange passing the ring of muscle, the plug was securely in place.

Never before had Amy felt so dirty and shameful. Even allowing Eric to do what he wanted to her wasn't nearly as humiliating.

Kali's fingers slid over Amy's moist mound. Finding her wet hole she slipped two fingers inside her.

Amy merely whimpered.

Spreading her labia wide, Kali leaned in and licked Amy's clit, seeming to enjoy watching her squirm. For what seemed like an hour, Kali's tongue teased her, working around her clit and occasionally plunging into the wet depths of her pussy.

"This is turning me on too much," Kali finally said. She began undressing, but not before grabbing her cell phone and dialing a number.

"Hi Eric. It's Kali. Oh I just thought I'd call you and tell you that you should come home for an hour. I have a lovely surprise for you." Her lilting voice stopped short and she cocked her head to one side, listening. "Well, let's just say I have your sub in a very compromising position and I'm getting ready to make her come. I thought I'd fuck her sweet little pussy with the double header I found."

Amy closed her eyes tightly, wanting to pull her thighs together to hide her arousal spurred by Kali's plan for her. But she couldn't. Her feet were in the stirrups of the table and her knees were held open by straps attached to bars on either side of the table.

"Well then I guess you better get home so you can properly punish both of us." Kali hung up with a satisfied smile and giggled. "I think poor Eric has just found himself exasperated. I fully intend on him coming home so he can watch."

Not sure what to do, Amy decided to go with dungeon protocol. "Mistress, I don't think this is a good idea…"

Kali slid her fingers up Amy's wet slit causing her to shove her hips forward instinctively. "I think it's a great idea." With that, Kali strapped on a dildo, turned on the vibrating butt plug, and plunged the dildo into Amy's dripping hole.

As Kali fucked her, she pulled at the clamps and chain binding Amy's breasts together. It was an odd, but wonderful sensation. Amy heard the door upstairs open and the footsteps coming through the house. Kali's fingers found Amy's clit and she started rubbing furiously. As Amy climaxed on the latex dildo she saw Eric standing there, watching.

Kali didn't make a move to stop or turn around. Instead, she kept doing what she was doing. "Tell Mistress Kali how you like her rubber cock in your pussy."

Amy's eyes went to Eric who gave her a nod. "Mistress Kali, I love having your rubber cock in my pussy."

"Good girl." She pulled it out and took off the strap on. "Welcome Master Eric."

"Okay, Kali, you've had your fun," Eric started.

Kali pouted at him. "I was just getting started. I was going to use that double header and perhaps teach her to eat pussy. Wouldn't you like to watch that?"

He shook his head. "Woman…I…"

"You know you want to. We won't keep you long. I just figured if there was some girl on girl action going on in your basement it was only fair you get to join in. It started innocently enough." Kali blinked at him.

Lifting an eyebrow he rolled his eyes. "Innocent my ass. You coerced her down here and somehow managed to get her tied up." His eyes traveled over Amy's bound and helpless body, pausing to note the vibrating butt plug in her ass. Then his eyes moved upward and settled on the nipple clamps. "Oh wow."

"Hot, right?" Kali smiled at him. "Once I saw them on her I couldn't resist."

"I'm thinking nipple clamps and some rope bondage," he said, unable to take his eyes off Amy's chest. The Dom inside Eric reared its head. "Kali, get Amy off the table and you get up there."

Kali stopped short and looked at him. "How did we go from rope bondage and nipple clamps to me up on the table?"

Without word, Eric took a flogger off the bench behind him. "Don't argue with me, woman. Do it or I'm going to give you a flogging you won't forget."

Kali stood stunned to silence, and then quickly went about undoing the restraints binding Amy to the table.

Amy hopped off the table carefully, wondering how much trouble she was going to be in when Eric finally got her alone. After all, she'd pretty much just cheated on him with a woman. A sinking feeling gripped her stomach.

With some reluctance Kali climbed up onto the table and laid back, putting her feet in the stirrups as Eric indicated with a nod of his head.

Eric gently took Amy by the arm and led her back toward the table. "Now Amy, I want you to please Mistress Kali with your tongue."

Kali smiled.

Amy didn't. She didn't know the first thing about licking a woman *down there*. She wasn't sure where to start.

Like usual, it was as if Eric read her mind. "Kali, you might have to tell Amy what to do. I don't think she's done this before."

"Well first, little Amy, slide your tongue up my slit, and then circle my clit with it," the Domme told her.

Leaning forward at the waist, she slipped her tongue into the crevice of Kali's pussy lips and licked upward, pulling her lips apart with her hands. When she found Kali's clit she ran her tongue around it and over it, and around it again. Kali smelled like pomegranates and spice and she tasted sweet and musky.

Kali let out a low groan. "That's it. Keep doing that."

Amy kept it up, sometimes sliding her tongue down to Kali's waiting hole and back up again.

Eric came up behind her. She felt his cock against her ass cheek, and then felt it push into her pussy. His hand reached around to rub her clit. He gently thrust his cock in and out of her. "Now slide three of your fingers into Mistress Kali's pussy," he ordered.

Amy did as instructed, shoving three fingers into the Domme as far as they would go. Kali was very wet. Ever so slowly she pulled her fingers out, and then pushed them back in, all while her tongue circled and sucked on Kali's clit. Kali's hands came down on Amy's head, holding her there while she shoved her hips forward, moaning.

Meanwhile Eric had built up a steady rhythm and kept thrusting his thick cock into her over and over again. He growled. "Make her come, baby."

Working her fingers in and out of Kali at a good clip, she found herself surprised at the sensation when Kali came. Her pussy spasmed against Amy's fingers. Amy gave in to the massaging of Eric's touch and she came, feeling her own muscles pulling and massaging his hard-on. With a few more vigorous thrusts, Eric buried himself deep inside her and enjoyed his own release.

Amy felt the butt plug stop vibrating. Eric had the controller now. Kali got up and disappeared into the bathroom to clean herself up. Eric eyed her cautiously. Amy looked down at her feet like a scolded child. "I'm sorry, Master, I didn't mean for it to happen..."

He didn't say anything for a moment.

This only caused her gut to wretch even more. She really liked Eric, she did. But clearly her libido was out of control and she was like a kid in a candy store. So many new experiences to choose from. "It's just I was curious," she started. "I mean, I've never intended... it started with the nipple clamps..."

Eric started laughing. "Relax. I know how it is. Besides, love, we never established any type of boundaries about being exclusive. I'm just happy you're experimenting with my friends and letting me in on it. However," his voice turned stern. "You did come into the dungeon without permission. So for the next four hours you will keep the butt plug in to remind you that you need to stay out of places you're told to stay out of." A small smile played on his lips.

"But Master, I..." she started to protest.

He put up a hand and shook his head. "Six hours. The more you protest the more I increase the time. You won't stay here, you'll go to classes and then you'll come to work." He held up the controller to the butt plug, turning it on, and then off again. "I fully intend on enjoying this punishment."

Then he took her by the hand, pulling her to him. His hand gently cupped her breast and he slid his fingers over her flesh. With practiced ease, he unclamped the left nipple. A shot of pain ran through Amy's breast.

"Ah!" she cried out.

"It's going to hurt, now hang on, I have to get the other one," he told her with a smile. He removed the other clamp quickly.

The sensation caused Amy to grab at her chest. Her nipple stung.

Eric gave her a nod. "Now go get cleaned up and get dressed, but I don't want you in jeans. I want you in a short skirt and heels. You have classes in twenty-five minutes, I'll drop you off."

Amy hurried past Kali, who'd evidently been standing there listening. From the bathroom she could hear Kali and Eric talking.

"I really didn't mean to get her in trouble with you Eric," Kali told him.

"Yes you did. Don't give me that innocent look. I know better Kali, you're wicked." He laughed. "I suspect you came over here for that specific reason."

"Well it wasn't fair that you and Brad were the only ones who got to play. Besides," she whispered, "We're all friends and she's damn cute. Not to mention I think she's good for you. You need a sub to keep you in line."

He laughed again. "Oh really?"

"Maybe some night we can do a foursome," she suggested.

"Three Doms on Amy, or would you switch sides for the night? Because *that* I'd like to see."

Amy finished up in the bathroom and came back into the dungeon, sweeping her clothes off the floor. She started pulling them on, acutely aware of the plug inside her. Once she was dressed she quietly followed Kali and Eric from the dungeon and back into the kitchen. First she ran upstairs to change from jeans to a mini-skirt with heels. Selecting a black skirt, panty hose and some black two inch heels didn't take long. Finally, grabbing her school bag, she silently followed Eric and Kali out of the house and got into the car while Eric saw Kali off. Then he drove her to the college and dropped her off.

She didn't get a lot from her class because she was too uncomfortable. There was that humiliating fear that everyone knew the large plug was in her ass by the way she walked, or it would slip out of her in public. Clenching tightly, the hour long class was a nightmare. Navigating stairs and curbs on her way to the bus stop was even more brutal. On the bus, the rough vibration of the seat caused the plug to feel large inside her and she felt herself getting aroused and wet. By the time she made it to the bookstore, she could feel how soaked her inner thighs were and she was terrified the wetness was dripping past her skirt.

Eric and Brad were talking about a book order when she came back behind the counter with her bag. She waited until they were done talking then asked Eric, "Can I please…"

He cut her off. "Not yet." He handed her a large stack of books. "Take these to romance and shelve them."

Giving him a small pout, she grabbed the books and started toward the shelves. When the plug came to life, humming inside her, she almost dropped the entire stack of books. Clenching and trying to pull her thighs together she made it to the stacks and started going through the books. She rolled her eyes. Eric had purposefully given her authors starting with 'T' meaning she'd have to lean down or kneel to shelve them, an interesting task while a large device vibrated in her anus. Carefully making sure the plug was where it should be, she carefully navigated to her knees, sat on her heels and began putting the books away. It was tempting to stay in that position because it felt so wonderful, but with no more books to put away she carefully got up, almost lost the plug, and had to resort to shoving it back inside her through her skirt and panties without anyone noticing. She carefully made her way back up to the counter and Eric. Luckily he was alone because Brad was helping a customer.

"Master, I apologize for going into the dungeon without permission. Can I please remove the butt plug now?"

"Now why would you want to do that, my little pet?" A small smile played on his lips.

"Because it's sliding out, Master," she whispered, absolutely humiliated.

"Brad, Amy and I are going to go move that inventory in back," Eric said.

Brad nodded and continued talking to the customer.

With a grateful sigh, Amy followed Eric into the back and into what she affectionately now called *the dungeon show room*.

"Take down your panties and lean over that bench," he ordered, pointing to the bench he meant.

Amy didn't even question, she did as she was told. Leaning over the bench she spread her legs, feeling the plug almost ready to slide out.

She heard Eric come up behind her, the rustle of a condom wrapper, and then she felt Eric pull on the plug. It slid out without any problems. "Nice. Just thinking about this butt plug stretching you out for me…" He ended the sentence with a growl.

With that she felt his cock press into her ass without any resistance. Her clit begged for attention, but she knew she likely wasn't going to get it. Eric liked torturing her; playing with her. Bringing her to the brink of orgasm and then stopping. It didn't take long for him to come. He pulled out of her, removing the condom and disposing of it in a discreet trash can. Then he took the plug and put in into a bath of cleaner in the utility sink.

Handing her a box of tissue he said, "Back to work gorgeous."

With that he disappeared from the room. She cleaned herself up, pulled her panties and hose back up, and then slipped her shoes back on. If anything she was grateful the plug had been removed. None worse for the wear, she went back to work as if nothing had happened at all.

Paul showed up at *By The Book* at eight that evening, just an hour before closing. Amy heard Brad intercept him.

"You need to leave," Brad told him.

"I just need to talk to Amy for a minute, out front. I just want to apologize, please man?" Paul said with more civility than she expected.

She ventured out from the shelves she was straightening and walked over to him. "Why are you here, Paul?"

He looked her up and down quickly, not quickly enough for it to go unnoticed. "I just want to talk to you outside for a minute. I want to apologize. I was way out of line the other night."

"I'll say you were," Amy said, leading him out to the front of the building.

Paul followed, his head down.

Once they were outside she turned to him, arms crossed over her chest. "Well, say what you have to say."

"Amy, I love you. Dump that guy. You deserve better. Do you know how many women into kinky sex get raped and murdered?" he asked. While his face showed concern, there was something angry about his eyes.

She tried not to wince. "Paul, we're done. I don't love you. I'm falling in love with Eric and our private life is our own. It's not up to you to judge it. I trust Eric would never let anything like that happen to me."

"Last year, in New York or someplace, a woman fell in love with a guy like Eric and he treated her like a queen until he auctioned her off as a sex slave in another country. Do you want to be another statistic?" Paul's voice was firmer now.

Amy paused for a moment. She had heard about it. It was a big story when it broke. "Eric isn't like that."

All the pleading and 'sorry' went from his face. "You really want men to beat you? Smack you around? You know what; I'm done trying to convince you. Obviously you've been brainwashed, so much you actually sent the cops looking into me for arson."

"That's what this is really about, isn't it? You're pissed because they're questioning you and not Eric." She shook her head in disbelief. "You're the only person I fought with, Paul. Who the hell do you think they're going to look into?"

"Yeah, well luckily I saw someone around your house that night."

Amy raised an eyebrow. "You what?"

"I keep an eye on what's mine. I saw some scrawny chick in gray hatchback follow you and Eric when he dropped you off. He left, she stuck around. I thought it was strange when she parked and walked over to the side of your house, but she came back, got in her car and left," he said with a shrug. "I thought maybe she was looking for a cat or something."

"God damn it Paul! Why didn't you say something sooner? Did you tell the police?" A rush of anger coursed through her.

"Of course I did. When they were questioning me I remembered it. I didn't think anything of it initially which is why I didn't say anything. So they think they have a lead." The look on his face showed a clear change in train of thought. "Am I back in your good graces now? Give me a second chance?"

She didn't answer him right away. Her mind was on the scrawny girl in the hatchback. Emily. "Oh God, it was Emily."

"Do I get a second chance or not?" Paul was asking.

Groaning, she looked him square in the eye. "No. Paul, I'm done with you."

"You want me to beat you?" he asked.

Shocked, she didn't say anything.

He grabbed her by the arm and began dragging her toward his car. "I'll beat you since that's what you like. I have a bullwhip back at my place. Come on."

Digging her heels into the ground and trying to pull away she shouted, "Paul, stop!" Anger gave way to fear.

"I thought you liked it rough? Come on, Amy. Give me a second chance."

"The lady said let go." It was Brad's voice.

Paul's grip loosened, giving Amy a chance to pull away and finally break free. She clutched her wrist and backed away. Eric came out of the store front door and stood next to Brad, motioning Amy to move closer to him.

"So what are you gonna do? Kick my ass? Do it," Paul said, shoving his nose only inches from Brad's face.

"No," Brad said, not losing an ounce of control. "But I will tell you what I *am* going to do. You're going to leave quietly or I'm calling the police and having you removed."

"This is a public sidewalk mother fucker!"

"And you're causing a public nuisance on the sidewalk in front of our store," Brad countered with a smile. "Take a hike."

"Amy, last chance. Me or Blondie there," Paul shouted.

"I'm staying with Eric, Paul. Now leave or I'll get a restraining order," she said, nursing her injured wrist.

Paul seemed to weigh his options then he let out a growl and stomped off toward his car, glaring back at them over his shoulder only once.

Inside, the last few customers of the night stood staring out the windows. One man was kind enough to ask Amy if she was alright.

"I'll be fine, thank you," she said politely. Going to the refrigerator she pulled out the ice pack and put it on her wrist, then went to sit at her place at the counter near the register.

Eric and Brad finally came back inside.

"Is prince charming gone?" she asked.

"I can't believe you dated that asshole," Brad said.

She laughed. "Neither can I."

"How's your wrist?" Eric asked, gently taking the ice pack off it and giving it close inspection.

"It feels bruised, maybe sprained," Amy said with a sigh.

"So how did that conversation go?" Eric obviously wanted details.

She wasn't about to let him down. "He told me something you're not going to like. Probably the most important thing that came out of his mouth."

He raised an eyebrow and said nothing.

"He told me that Sunday night when you brought me home, when he was stalking me evidently, he noticed we were being followed by a gray hatchback driven by a scrawny brown haired chick, who after I went inside and you drove away, got out of her car and went to the side of my parents' house, then got back in her car and left. Then he left," Amy said with a tight smile.

"Emily?" Eric asked, the shock clear in his voice.

"Yes. Your psycho ex tried to kill me and my parents."

"She's off her meds," he whispered.

"She's on meds?"

"She's on anti-psychotics. She's got a mild form of schizophrenia."

Amy was speechless. Evidently Emily was more damaged than anyone had been willing to admit.

"I can't believe you dated that crazy bitch," Brad said, walking by with a stack of books.

"He told the cops, right?" Eric asked.

"He said he did. Then he offered to take me back to his place and beat me with a bull whip since I like to be beaten," she said with a sigh. "What a jerk. I should get a restraining order because…"

Eric didn't let her finish. "Let's go file a report now."

"Sure," Brad said in a sarcastic tone as he came back around the counter. "I'll close the store while you two run off. Thank God you both stopped dating assholes and started dating each other."

Eric and Amy both laughed. Eric was right. Brad actually did have a sense of humor after all.

Chapter Ten

It was a cold, gray day two months later when they got the news that Emily had been arrested for arson and attempted murder. She had been off her meds, so they said. Amy and Eric were at the DA's office giving their statements when Amy ran into her parents who immediately scowled at Eric. He excused himself and wandered down the hall, acting like he was interested in getting something from the vending machine.

"We've rented a house near your aunt's," her mother started.

"That's great," Amy said, forcing a grin.

"We want you to move back in with us while you finish school."

"Thanks for the offer, Mom, but I think I'm going to stay with Eric," she said.

Her father walked away.

Her mother looked at her. "Amy, we're worried about you."

"You heard I had to get a restraining order against Paul? He bruised my wrist and threatened to beat me with a bull whip when I refused to take him back," Amy said, her voice bitter.

"Oh Amy, I'm so sorry." She reached out to take Amy's hand. "We just want the best for you and we don't want to see you get hurt or drop out of school over some man."

"Eric hasn't hurt me, mom. I know you don't believe it, but he treats me with respect and we have a lot in common. We both like to read, watch the same movies, and have the same work ethic. He's also adamant about me finishing school. I haven't missed a day since I've been staying with him," she assured her. "Besides, he's got a big place and he needed a roommate anyway."

"Oh, so you're not sharing a bedroom?"

Amy fought the urge to roll her eyes. "No mother. I have my own room," she lied. The lie was worth it though because that put a smile on Mrs. Meyer's face and the conversation ended there with her mother agreeing to call her and have her over for dinner. No mention was made of inviting Eric, but Amy reminded herself it was going to take small baby steps for her parents to get used to the idea that first, she was a grown woman, and second she'd chosen a man and a lifestyle they didn't approve of. But it was a risk Amy was fully prepared to take.

With that agreement, Amy left her parents, rejoined Eric and they headed home.

When they pulled into the driveway at the house a half hour later and Amy looked up at the two story monstrosity before her, then over at Eric whose eyes almost always gave him away, she knew she was home with the man she was falling deeper in love with by the day.

"So since we have the rest of the day and Brad and Kali have the shop under control, how about we take the opportunity to have a play date?" he suggested with a wide grin. Then he leaned over and kissed her, hard, running his hand over her clothed breast. He pulled back, looking into her eyes, seemingly waiting for her answer.

A small smirk crossed her lips. "I don't know, Master. I thought I'd paint my nails."

"Mouthy are we? That deserves punishment. Perhaps you'll serve me the rest of the day nude, on your hands and knees with a ball gag in your mouth? I think that sounds absolutely delicious," he said in a husky whisper.

Her breath hitched and she found herself immediately aroused by idea. "Yes, Master. Whatever you wish."

He firmly, yet gently, pulled her to him again, kissing her full on the lips, his tongue exploring her mouth. He pulled away again, this time his eyes filled with lust. "Now get inside and get naked. You'll wear the cuffs, too," he told her.

With her panties wet and her every pore craving his command, needing to serve him, her voice came out small and wanting. "Yes, Master." •

To read more of Brad and Kali's story, watch for *Switched* by Anne O'Connell. Coming Soon!

More BDSM Erotica by Anne O'Connell

Her Demon Lover (coming in 2011)

Lori Penhall is a bit wary when she inherits her great uncle's estate in Ireland. After all, she didn't know him. Leaving Akron and her ex-husband behind, she travels to County Galway to look over her recently acquired property, fully intending to sell it. That is until she meets the handsome dark and mysterious Michael O'Siad who rents the renovated castle on the grounds. One night he invites her to a private "dungeon" party. Intrigued by what she sees but mortified by how it makes her feel, Michael shows Lori what it means to truly be free. She begins to fall in love with him, only to learn he has other dark, intriguing secrets - darker than a "working" dungeon. Will his secrets tear them apart, or will their love and desire for each other be enough to keep them together?

Publisher's Note: This book contains explicit sexual content, graphic language, and situations that some readers may find objectionable: BDSM theme and content includes: dubious consent, bondage, spanking, anal play, voyeurism, and ménage m/f/m.

My Neighbor Enslaved (coming in 2011)

Brittney Cavenaugh has a sexy neighbor named Bruce who she can't stop watching and fantasizing about. After she meets him at a block picnic and he offers to be her on-call handyman she immediately whips up some chores for him to do. Can she convince him to let her tie him up and have her way with him?

Publisher's Note: This book contains explicit sexual content, graphic language, and situations that some readers may find objectionable: BDSM theme and content includes: femDom, bondage, spanking and anal play.

Weekend Captive

Kate's track record with men has been lousy. Now, she's sworn off them for good. But someone has other ideas.

He's been watching Kate go about her days indifferent to him and any other man who crosses her path. Tired of being ignored and unable to cage the burning desire within, he has a plan to make her his...

When Kate wakes up blindfolded and bound she knows she has a new set of problems. Will she be able to escape with her life?

Publisher's Note: This book contains explicit sexual content, graphic language, and situations that some readers may find objectionable: BDSM theme and content includes: dubious consent, bondage, spanking, toys, anal play, and ménage m/f/m.

Nice Girls Don't

Jenny has never led an exciting life. Everything from her interests to her looks are ordinary. Even her sex life is dull. That is until she and her boyfriend Darek agree to a night of exploration at a BDSM club with friends. While there, Jenny learns that Darek has a dark secret he's been keeping from her and even more than that - she has a submissive side that yearns to be dominated. Will her resistance destroy her and Darek's relationship, or will she give in to her carnal desires?

Publisher's Note: This book contains explicit sexual content, graphic language, and situations that some readers may find objectionable: BDSM theme and content includes: bondage, spanking, toys, anal play, voyeurism, and ménage m/f/m.

SINcerely, Megan

Megan's imagination and libido are out of control. She just can't stop fantasizing about Father Michaels. So when she steps into his confessional just to be closer to him and confesses all her sinful thoughts, she's surprised when Father Michaels offers her private counseling. Little does she know what Father Michaels has in store for her and it's nothing she could have imagined. The priest also has a secret past, one he thought he left behind him when he entered the priesthood. Will they be able to cage their lust or will the transgression ruin both their lives forever?

Publisher's Note: This book contains explicit sexual content, graphic language, and situations that some readers may find objectionable: BDSM theme and content includes: bondage, spanking, toys, anal play, and masturbation.

About the Author

Anne O'Connell lives with her husband and numerous animal companions. She enjoys the taboo, the profound, the surreal, and the macabre. When she isn't writing erotic bdsm fiction (not for the faint of heart) she enjoys long walks in the park, watching the sunset, drinking coffee as the sun rises, and romantic nights out. Anne is the author of Midnight Fantasy Press titles *SINcerely Megan*, *Nice Girls Don't*, *Weekend Captive*, *Training Amy* and the forthcoming *My Neighbor Enslaved* and *Her Demon Lover*. Find her fan page on Facebook to keep up with current and upcoming releases!